BAD CONNECTION

ALSO BY MICHAEL LEDWIDGE

The Narrowback

Available in paperback from Pocket Books

BAD CONNECTION

Michael Ledwidge

POCKET BOOKS

NEW YORK   LONDON   TORONTO   SYDNEY   SINGAPORE

This book is a work of fiction. Names, characters, places and incidents are products of the author's imagination or are used fictitiously. Any resemblance to actual events or locales or persons, living or dead, is entirely coincidental.

 Pocket Books, a division of Simon & Schuster, Inc.
1230 Avenue of the Americas, New York, NY 10020

Library of Congress Cataloging-in-Publication Data

Ledwidge, Michael.
    Bad connection / Michael Ledwidge.
        p. cm.
    ISBN 0-7434-0593-5
    1. Telephone companies—Employees—Fiction. 2. Chief
executive officers—Fiction. 3. Consolidation and merger of
corporations—Fiction. 4. Manhattan (New York, N.Y.)—
Fiction. I. Title.

PS3562.E316 B33 2001
813'.54—dc21   00-049129

First Pocket Books hardcover printing April 2001

10 9 8 7 6 5 4 3 2 1

Designed by Jaime Putorti

Printed in the U.S.A.

*For the men of Midtown Cable Maintenance
who go down in a hole every day and manage to
climb back out.*

SUMMER

CHAPTER ONE

SEAN MACKLIN PULLED his phone truck over to the corner of Forty-second and Lexington only after the third time Control had beeped him. The first summons, he knew, could've been just an all-points beep-out for some crappy job for the first sucker who called in. The second beep he could deny ever getting. But the third time his Motorola buzzed, and his boss's number appeared in the display box with the disheartening suffix 911, he was forced to pay it some heed.

He put the truck in park and got out, leaving it running. He stepped to the pay phone. He had a cell phone in his bag in the truck, but he knew not to use it. If his foreman learned he had a cell, he'd never have peace again. He dropped a quarter and dialed.

"Frank?" he said when it was picked up.

"He's in the can," a voice said. "You wanna call back or wait?"

Macklin took a breath.

"Hold, here I come," he said.

He looked up Forty-second. It was almost eight, and rich business types from Westchester and Connecticut were spilling out of Grand Central, their watches and shoes and brass briefcase clasps glinting in the sun.

Macklin looked at their new clothes and tans, their intent steps. Most seemed happy this late-summer morning, as if each were the star of his own show and turn-of-the-century Manhattan was the thrilling backdrop. Their bemused eyes went right through him as they walked past. Of course, he thought, he didn't warrant a glance. He just worked on the scenery. He was one of the key grips.

Macklin dug the plastic pay phone receiver into the crook of his neck and fished out a well-thumbed paperback from the side pocket of his coveralls.

He opened it at random.

Every person is given at least one opportunity to become successful, he read. *The object is to be ready to capitalize when that opportunity presents itself.*

"I'm ready," he said.

"Sean?" a voice said on the line.

"I don't want to work overtime, Frank," Macklin said. "I'm late as it is."

"Jesus, Sean. Relax yourself," said his boss. "Where the fuck you been anyway? I been beeping you for an hour."

"Over on Lex. You know how signals bounce around these glass canyons."

"'Bounce around,' my ass," Frank said.

"As tempting as that sounds, Frank," Macklin said, smiling, "I gotta get out of here. I'm already running late."

"Take you five minutes. Run by Eleven ninety-two Sixth and find out if cable twenty-two thirty-four terminates there. Griffin got some kind of fucked-up loop goin' on. I don't know what the hell he's done."

Macklin took out a pen and scribbled on the inside cover of the book.

"One-one-nine-two and two-two-three-four?"

"Uh-huh."

"You're the boss," Macklin said.

It took two minutes to drive to the building three blocks up and three over on Sixth and Forty-fifth. It was a fifty-story office tower of glass and steel set back from the avenue behind two half-block-long fountains. He parked in front, reached beneath his seat, and lifted out what looked like a telephone receiver. Clipping the dial set to his belt loop, he opened the truck door and got out.

More suits were on the sidewalk. They eyed Macklin and his dusty lead-splattered coveralls skeptically as he walked with them between the still fountains to the revolving door. Inside, the lobby was thirty feet high and encased in green marble. The rumble of shoes on polished stone, mixed with the dinging of the elevator doors, echoed out loudly in the high-ceilinged chamber like the sound of a massive cash register. He walked up to the security desk, took out his wallet, and showed his ID.

"Gotta get down to your phone room," he said.

He signed his name in a book, and the guard pointed to a door. It opened into a descending puke green stairwell that was thick with hot air. Macklin hadn't been in this particular building before, but he knew the drill. They stood on less ceremony in the back rooms and basements. He wiped his forehead and dropped his eyes, scanning for rats.

The phone room was better than he'd expected. The wall-to-wall steel frame that held the posts of all the building's phone lines was clear. Some high-speed data muxing consoles blinked along a wall. At least they didn't use it as a storeroom, he thought. There was nothing like trying to get a hundred customers back in service cramped between clothing racks or squeezed on top of boxes.

He took out his paperback and checked the 2234 cable number he'd written against the "CABLE 2234" written in marker along the top of the frame.

Well, what do you know, he thought. One of the records up in the control center actually matched something in the field.

He held his dial set in the crook of his neck and clipped its leads across the random twin posts of a line to call back his foreman.

"So how does it feel being twenty-six and about to become a multimillionaire?" said a voice.

"Well, it feels—" a young voice said in reply. "It, um, it feels real good, Speed. Real good."

Macklin became very still. He could feel his heartbeat very distinctly. Relax and contract. Relax and contract.

"Now, you guys literally started this company out of your garage?" the first, smooth voice was saying.

"Well, um, it was a barn actually. We were renting this farmhouse outside of Syracuse after we graduated and there was this barn and we worked out of there."

It was okay to use a line when you were working on it, Macklin knew, but if someone was on it, you were supposed to disengage. He glanced at his book.

Every person is given at least one opportunity to become successful.

A bead of sweat dripped off the ridge of his temple and made a small dark circle in the dust of the cement floor.

The object is to be ready to capitalize when that opportunity presents itself.

He held his breath and pressed the receiver in closer to his ear.

"What are you guys trading at right now?"

"Right now, eight and a quarter," the younger man said. "Yeah, eight and a quarter."

"Do you know what American Internet is trading at?"

"Close to two hundred, isn't it?"

"One ninety-seven and a third."

"Jeez," the kid said.

"After the takeover, your stake will translate somewhere in the neighborhood of two hundred and seventy million, Tim."

Macklin felt like he'd just been zapped with an electric charge. Tim whistled.

"I don't know what to say."

Macklin's knee began bobbing up and down.

The name of your company, he thought.

Please God, say the name of your company.

"How did you guys come up with 'Palomino' anyway? There were horses on the farm?"

Palomino, Macklin mouthed. His hand was shaking as he wrote it in the back of his book. Palomino. Palomino.

"Nah, it was a joke. The landlord's wife had this long face, bucked teeth, and a ponytail. We called her the Palomino."

"Boys will be boys," Speed said. "Well, congratulations, Tim. You deserve it. So that's Tuesday at nine at the Waldorf. Suite eleven-oh-six. I'll see you then, okay? Oh, and remember, don't purchase any Palomino stock between now and Tuesday, okay? Last thing we want is to make the SEC nervous, all right? Again, congratulations, Mr. Truman."

"Gee thanks, Mr. Ang . . . I mean, Speed. Thanks a lot. See you then."

"Bye-bye," Speed said.

They both hung up.

Macklin listened to dial tone for a while. Then he pulled the leads of his dial set off the posts of the line with a double snip. He looked down at the battleship gray floor.

Too good to be true, he thought. No way. It'll be some type of practical joke or something.

Palomino, he thought.

He'd have to find out.

He quickly wrapped up the dial set, clipped it back to the belt of his coveralls, and jogged out the phone room door. He jogged up the stairs and took out his notebook as he approached the security desk. The white-haired guard looked up.

"What's up, guy?" Macklin said. He looked at his notebook. "Does a Speed somebody or other got an office in this building?"

"Speed Angstrom?" the guard said.

"Maybe. Is he an investment banker?"

The guard hit some keys on the terminal in front of him.

"Uh," the guard said, reading, "he's the head of Mergers and Akwa—akwa—"

"Acquisitions?"

"That's it."

"Which company?"

The guard gestured with his chin at the marble wall. Macklin turned to the golden bull hanging there. Huge muscles stood out in the bull's neck as if it had just busted through the majestic stone from the street. Even he knew it was the logo of one of the most prestigious investment firms in the country.

"First Investment," the guard said.

Macklin felt light suddenly, helium filled, as if he'd start to float.

"Why? Something wrong with his phone?" the guard said.

Macklin looked with effort at his blank page.

"Ah, I don't even know. The information my boss gave me is all fucked up. I work nights for christsake. I'm supposed to be outta here already."

The guard rubbed at his own tired eyes.

"Tell me about it, brother," he said. "I'm working a double right now myself."

Macklin nodded sympathetically with fierce effort. He needed to be on the Internet right now.

"Ah, I think I'll just let the day crew pick it up," Macklin said, taking a measuredly casual step toward the revolving doors.

"That's what I'd do," the guard replied.

Macklin didn't start running until he got past the fountains. He left the truck where it was and ran down Sixth toward the library, where there was public Internet access. He'd gone two blocks when he remembered the library didn't open until eleven. Out of the corner of his eye, he spotted the

CYBER LATTE sign across the street. Horns wailed as he ran into the rush-hour traffic.

It was dark inside, and there was some weird New Age music playing. A line of impatient-looking executives with metallically textured shirts and ties waited by the counter. There were tables in the back with monitors on top of them. He stepped to an empty table, cleared the screen, and typed in the address of his stock-trading Web site. He'd just typed "Palomino.com" into the research section when he felt a presence at his elbow.

It was a short, odd-looking humanoid, possibly female in origin, with severely cut black hair and thick, square eyeglasses. He watched her nose wrinkle. He knew what she smelled. He'd been ladling molten lead on a damaged telephone cable in a dank Fifth Avenue manhole all night long.

He leaned toward her. She took a step back.

"Hi," he said.

"Only customers are allowed access to our terminals," she said.

"I'll take a coffee," he said.

The side of her mouth twitched down.

"Fine," she said. "We have Moroccan Tradewinds, Kilimanjaro Supreme . . ."

He looked back as the screen changed. Palomino was a two-year-old book-and-CD Web company that was considered culturally savvy, he read. It was hip, upscale, another Amazon.com.

"Sir?"

He thought the last thing she'd said sounded like "la monde" or something. He would've asked her if it was French for "chock full of nuts," but he didn't have time.

"What?" he said

"Which coffee?"

"First one sounds great," he said, without looking at her.

"For sizes, we have short, small, medium—"

"Supersize it," he said.

He brought up his trading account. There was five grand there from his retirement savings. All the stories he'd heard and read about people getting rich by doing their own investing had appealed to him. He'd taken some money out of his mutual fund and been screwing around with it. He'd been trading for a month, and his account was up a couple of hundred bucks. He wasn't sure if that was better or worse than what the pros managed. But what he had learned was that when one company took over another, the stock-holders in the company getting taken over made a bundle of money.

He typed up a five-thousand-dollar purchase order of Palomino stock at the opening price. Then he crossed his fingers and clicked *submit.*

The waitress brought his coffee and the check as he was clearing the screen. Even though it was $4.79, he didn't say a thing. He put a five on the table, picked up the coffee, and left.

Outside the sun was full up. Light flooded down the side streets and lay in white stripes across the avenue. He could feel the temperature rising already, the night cool long gone. He crossed the crowded street and walked to his truck. He opened its door and sat. Errant executives and pretty sneaker-clad secretaries scurried quickly in the buildings' shadows like actors heading for their places before the curtain's rise. He looked out at the building he'd just been under. Most of it was still a stark, shadowed glass form, but when he craned his neck, he could see the dazzling sparkle of the sunlight that licked its upper floors.

He winced at the first sip of the expensive coffee. It tasted like hot perfume. He got out and chucked it into the trash can on the corner. He ordered another coffee from the doughnut cart there. The Arab behind the shiny aluminum counter smiled widely as he handed it over to him.

"You look happy, my friend," he said. "Just hit Lotto?"

Macklin gazed out at the brand-new day and grinned.

"Something like that," he said.

FALL

CHAPTER TWO

"WE COULD GO hostile, you know, Robert."

Robert Brent rapped his heavy West Point ring on the dark wood surface of his desk and swiveled impatiently in his leather chair. Something in the caller's voice, the nasal inflection perhaps, irked him.

"If the company is as undervalued as you say, it might make more sense," the voice said.

Brent gazed out his wide, floor-to-ceiling window thirty-two stories above Park Avenue, giving the suggestion some thought.

"Absolutely not," he said finally.

"If it's a question of financing?" His delivery was as smooth as varnished mahogany. He was a Wasp, a thirty-four-year-old mergers-and-acquisitions head by the name of Speed

Angstrom. *Speed*, Brent thought, irritated. That wasn't even a name. That was something you did when you were running late.

"We want a friendly merger," Brent said. "Emphasis on the 'friendly.' We're not corporate raiders, Speed. We're scientists."

"Just apprising you of your options, Robert," Speed said.

Go hostile, Brent thought, the balls. He recalled Speed from his picture in *Money* magazine. The blond hair and suspenders, the smug, rakish smile. Did people even do hostile takeovers anymore? He'd hired First Investment to do a merger, but Speed was telling him to go takeover. Besides being unseemly, hostile takeovers were risky, at best, for the company doing the seizing, Brent knew. Investment bankers loved them because they made money no matter what the outcome.

"Well, we're just looking for a dull merger," Brent said.

"Point made," Speed conceded.

Who the hell did he sound like? Brent thought. Then it came to him. Thurston Howell III, from *Gilligan's Island*. A young Thurston Howell.

Point made, Lovey, my dear.

"We'll kick Allied down to our analyst," Speed continued, "and see what kind of initial numbers he can come up with for the tender. How solid are you at this point?"

"Everyone seems to be in agreement except our board, which convenes today," Brent told him. "But I'm very confident that we'll be getting the green light."

"You want me to be there?"

"Thanks, but we don't want to seem too eager just yet. I'll call you as soon as it's through," Brent told him.

"All right, then. Talk to you later," the banker said, and hung up.

Yeah, Brent thought. Say hi to the professor and Mary Ann, you pompous . . . Brent stopped himself. He put the receiver down and glanced at his steel Rolex. Five to eleven. Gotta get moving. He hit the intercom on the black-and-silver phone on his desk.

"Suzie, get Sam for me."

"Sure thing, Mr. Brent."

Brent stood, rolled his neck, and stretched. It was nervy work, this deal making. He'd thought the day-to-day operations were tough. It would be worth it, though, he reminded himself, once it was all said and done.

The board was the problem. They treated the slightest policy change like you were amending the Constitution. It was nearly impossible to keep Chemtech competitive when they prevented his every move.

They flat out had no grasp of the speed with which technology was changing now, the possibilities that were being presented. There was too much focus on the Internet. Every day, it was Internet this and Internet that and twenty-five-year-old programmers becoming billionaires. The Internet was a hoax, an electronic flea market. The real-world applications of all these technological advances in computer science, he knew, would be in biology and chemistry. If the twentieth century had been about physics, the experts predicted the twenty-first would be about biology. A shift in the paradigm was coming, and it was Brent's desire to position Chemtech at its forefront.

He'd been scouting around and had come across a small biotech company, Allied Genesis, that seemed to be just what he'd been looking for. State-of-the-art equipment, brilliant scientific staff, forward-thinking management. And when he'd taken a tour of their labs out in Jersey three weeks earlier, he'd seen something there that had instantly solidified his choice.

"Mr. Weiss on line one," his secretary piped in.

"Robert, what can I do for you?" a mellow, older voice asked when he lifted up the receiver.

Brent smiled. Sam Weiss was Chemtech's general counsel and his most trusted confidant.

"Just a couple of things before the meeting, Sam. I just got off the phone with First Investment," Brent told him.

"What did they say?" Sam asked.

"We should go hostile."

"Figures," Sam said. "It's like going to a plastic surgeon to get stitches taken out. Before you know it, you're hooked up to the liposuction machine and you're getting your nose redone. What did you tell him?"

"We weren't in the market. We're not, right?"

"I'd say no at this point, but let's leave it as an option if the board bristles about a merger."

"I hadn't thought of that. You think the board might look at a takeover more kindly?"

"Well, they could see a merger as a threat."

Brent lifted a pen off his desk and began twirling it in his fingers.

"I thought takeovers were cutthroat. You think we could stomach a takeover?" he said.

"It depends. How badly do you want this company? Is what you saw at Allied worth it?"

"Sam, this enzyme at Allied, it acts like a dehalogenase, but it's different. It—"

"Jesus, in English, Robert. Please."

"Sam, it breaks down toxic chemicals like nothing I've ever seen. I described it to R and D, and they said if we can combine it—and they're ninety-nine percent sure we can—with the new protein our labs came up with this summer, we're looking at something special, a real breakthrough. If the *Exxon Valdez* had what we think we're going to have, there wouldn't have been a problem. And the crazy part is, Allied was trying to apply it to cancer research, but it didn't work. Can you believe it? The synergy that's going to be generated once we get this thing up and running? I'm really excited."

"It's your call then, Robert. If you do go takeover and Allied gets wind of it, you could lose it. How receptive is Allied at this point?"

"Well, Allied's head, Ted Phillips, is pro-environment. Initially, he seemed hesitant to get into bed with us hard-chemical monsters, but at lunch with him on Friday, I reassured him of his place in our new venture. He called me this morning. He's in."

Sam was silent for a moment.

"I'd say merger then, Robert. You catch more flies with honey. Just make sure you hammer home the importance of this breakthrough enzyme at the meeting. And use lots of graphs. You know how much they like graphs."

Brent looked at his watch.

"Oh, I'm all set, Sam. I've even got a new laser pointer."

"You should've said so in the first place," Sam said. Brent could hear the smile in his voice. "It's a done deal then."

"Thanks, buddy," Brent said.

"Anytime. See you in ten," Sam said, and hung up.

Brent smiled as he laid the phone back in its cradle. He

was glad Sam had recognized Allied's enzyme as a main point in selling the merger to the board. If there was anything being pumped up, it was the enzyme's true possibility. It would be useful in some applications, but it wasn't half as revolutionary as he purported. The enzyme was just the carrot that would move the reluctant board into the future. But if old Sam had bought it, Brent thought, then the board would jump with both feet.

Brent stood and stepped to the small washroom off his office. He looked at himself in the mirror over the sink.

He was a tall, handsome man with straight black hair and striking gray eyes. A young, fit forty. In his new razor-cut navy Brioni suit, he looked imposingly professional. He had to, as Chemtech's youngest-ever CEO.

Industrial chemical companies were usually headed by old men, iron-fisted skeletons in three-piece suits. That's what good ol' Speed didn't understand. He thought he was impressive because he was thirty-four and the head of a department in an investment bank. But he worked on Wall Street, where they didn't care how old you were as long as you made them money. Brent worked in hard chemicals, where they wanted their heads to be as invariable and caustic as the chemicals their companies produced. To be where he was at forty was a much harder goal to attain than where Speed was at thirty-four.

He was going to splash water on his face, but then decided he didn't need to. He clicked off the light and walked back out to his desk.

He stared out his window at the glass faces and razor corners of the other office towers. Beyond them, the faded iron and brick of the tenements and old factories across the East

River stood out pale and faded in the late morning light. He stood there, taking in the vista of raw urban sprawl. Standing before it up this high felt dangerous, he thought, like being dangled over a bed of nails. He decided it was a feeling he liked.

Just one more hurdle now, he thought. He checked his watch. Then he stood and walked for the door.

The walls of the boardroom were made of glass. It was an "inclusive space," explained the architect who'd redone the offices. Approaching it with his career on the line and seeing the entire board, seated around the runway-long table of light-colored wood, swing their eyes toward him in unison, Brent thought maybe that term wasn't as attractive as it had first sounded. He felt a pang of panic well up as he opened the glass door, but by the time he made it to the head of the table by the graphs, it was already gone.

IT TOOK THIRTY minutes after his presentation for the decision. He was sitting at his desk, staring out the window when Suzie buzzed in the board president.

President Gitta Shutz was a prim, squat woman in her sixties. She came right to the point.

"You have our approval," she said. "With one condition."

Brent masked his triumph.

"What's that?" he said.

"We'll approve the merger, but only if it's inexpensive. As both stocks are trading pretty closely, a one-for-one stock swap should be sufficient. We won't get into any bidding wars, so you'd better make sure this is a solid, quick transaction."

"All right. Is that all?"

"That's all," she said, smiling. "Congratulations, Robert."

Brent allowed himself a wide smile back at her.

"No, it's you guys who deserve the congratulations. I'm really happy to see that you're embracing this. You and the stockholders won't be disappointed."

"I should hope not," the president said as she went for the door.

He waited until the door completely closed before he thought, *Eighty million.*

He'd pulled it off!

Eighty million.

Eighty million was the compensation that Speed had set up for his stock options as part of the deal. And why not? These Internet people were making billions on companies that were barely solvent. Why shouldn't he get paid a fraction of that for running a company that made a respectable profit every quarter? One that would be a global force to reckon with in the coming century. Allied was just the first in a series of acquisitions he envisioned. Pharmaceuticals would be next, perhaps a health-care provider. It was going to work, he thought, amazed.

In the two years before he'd been made CEO, he'd been sorely tempted many times to jump ship to a dot-com. He had the résumé, and the compensation to be made with stock options was irresistible.

But he'd stopped himself. Perhaps it was loyalty, perhaps a distaste for leaving his work undone. He'd held on. And now . . . and now . . .

Eighty million.

His nut.

Finally.

Brent speed-dialed Sam.

The old lawyer answered.

"We did it!!!" Brent yelled.

"Great news, Robert. Really great. When? Just now?"

"Just this very moment. I can't believe we pulled it off, old buddy. Thanks for all your help."

"What am I here for?" Sam asked jovially. "I'm so pleased for you. You really deserve this, Robert. I'm very happy. When do we celebrate?"

"Soon, Sam. And let me tell you something, Sam. This is just the beginning."

"Did you tell the bankers yet?"

"What? I'm gonna tell those sharks before you? I have to call Phillips first, anyway. The only thing about this is, we have to keep the lid on very tight. One of the conditions of the board's agreement was a one-for-one stock swap. That looks like a decent offer right now, but if there's any play in Allied's stock, we won't be able to afford her."

"You make sure you let Speed know that," Sam said.

"I will, Sam. Thanks again."

"Take care."

Brent hung up.

Suzie piped in.

"Mr. Brent? There's a Mr. Guest on line two."

Guest? Brent thought. Oh, yes, he remembered quickly. El Salvador.

They'd moved a pesticide plant to Central America recently, and they'd been having some trouble. It was the same old story. Though they'd placed the plant in a jungle area so as to affect the least number of people, even in that remote section of the world, there was some indigenous tribe that hadn't been happy with their presence. Claims had been made that Chemtech was poisoning the land and streams. There'd been protests, vandalism, theft. And when a small fire had been set three weeks ago, it was Guest who'd contacted Brent with suggestions for smoothing over the problem. That's what this must be about.

Strange, though, Brent thought. He'd distinctly told Guest to report in future to the office of the Central American division head.

"Tell him to speak to—" Brent started.

"He says he can't speak to anyone but you, Mr. Brent. He's very insistent about it."

"Very well," Brent said. "Put him through."

"Mr. Brent?" a voice said.

"Mr. Guest. How can I help you?"

"We have a problem," Guest said urgently. "Are you alone?"

"Yes, I'm alone. What is it?"

"Is this line secure?"

What the? Brent thought. Something turned in his stomach, a dropping sensation.

"On this end it is. Why?"

"There's been an incident involving the protesters."

"What?"

"Two days ago, I sat down with the local governor and explained our situation. Last night, a troop truck went up into the protesters' village. There was a shooting."

Brent convulsed in his seat.

"People are dead," Guest said.

For the glorious love of God.

"Could you—" Brent said, "could you repeat that for me?" he said.

"Thirty or forty people, Mr. Brent. That's what I can

gather so far. I know it's a shock. There's more. I got a call from the district governor this morning. He made the suggestion that we should give him a bonus for solving the problem."

"Jesus Christ," Brent cried. "A bonus?"

"He made implications about the press, getting Chemtech's name embroiled. This is the bonus he's talking about."

"A payoff?!" Brent asked.

"That's about the size of it."

"Even though his troops did it?!"

"This is a pretty backward district down here, Mr. Brent. The governor's been cited by Amnesty International and others. He laughs at them. He doesn't care about human rights."

"Why didn't you tell me about this before?" Brent yelled.

There was a long pause from Guest.

"I don't remember you asking about that sort of thing. What I do remember is you calling me twice a day about how quickly approvals for the plant's construction could be granted. If you want, I could call back later," Guest said. "Or perhaps you'd like me to call the Central American district head. I believe you gave me his number."

Brent swallowed. He was at the business agent's mercy, and they both knew it.

"I'm sorry. Continue," Brent said.

"There is one positive thing."

Brent closed his eyes; an image of soldiers firing machine guns into grass huts appeared to him.

"What's that?"

"I believe if we pay, this will disappear."

"How much?"

There was another pause from Guest.

"Two million," he said.

"Hold a moment," Brent said.

Brent put Guest on hold and held the receiver to his forehead.

Of all the times, he thought. No. He cut himself off. The correct decision had to be made. He calculated quickly: the consequences, the rewards, the risk. He tapped his ring against the desk. He remembered being told a long time ago that a leader had to be ready to quit at any moment. That moment, he realized, was upon him.

He simply could not go back to square one.

He would not. He got back on the line.

"Do whatever's necessary, Mr. Guest," he said decisively. "Make this go away. We're right in the midst of a major merger. Two million and not a dime more. Use the account in Mexico City. And let me hear from you soon."

"I'll call you," Guest said.

Brent hung up. He turned toward the window, searching a vista that had so frequently brought inspiration. In the distance, he watched the horizon shift almost imperceptibly. Perhaps a high wind had set a slight sway to the upper floors of the tower.

Eighty million, he thought. He could feel it slipping through his fingers.

He stood and took a step back from the window, his mind racing to catch up to his hammering heart.

CHAPTER THREE

IN THE DARKNESS, the letters and numbers marched. Sean Macklin gazed through the dusty windshield of his phone truck as they streamed tirelessly across the black face of the digital sign above. Their yellow light flickered over his face. A block down Broadway in Times Square, stronger light from the Jumbotrons and cliff-sized neon billboards blazed like an electric bonfire, but Macklin hardly noticed them. He had a small notebook open in his lap and a pen in his hand. The radio was on. He listened to it.

"And in the M-and-A world, New York–based pharmaceutical giant NOVA merged today with the lesser-known Dutch company Van Hollins Holdings in a four-and-a-half billion-dollar deal. NOVA CEO, Michael Burchetta, will retain leadership. Rumors of a well-known American chemical company in the market for a biotech wing still persist, but which chem giant and which biotech are answers this reporter wished she knew. This is Patricia Carter for Market Radio, all money, all the time. At the beep, the time will be twelve mid—"

Macklin clicked off the radio as a young man emerged from the candy store across the street. He had the notebook put away by the time the passenger door opened.

"Black, two sugars?" the young man said. He was a skinny kid with long hair and was wearing a black Metallica T-shirt under his army coat. His name was Puckett. Macklin took the coffee and dropped the truck into drive.

"Thanks a lot," he said.

They drove down through the pulsing square. The theaters were still letting out, and the surging crowds of people on the sidewalks were black and backlit against the glow. The two men drove past where the ball dropped on New Year's Eve and continued a few blocks and made a right. They rolled a block west and turned onto dark Eighth. In the middle of the avenue, Macklin slowed and flicked on the truck's emergency strobes. He scanned the patched roadway. The headlights caught the dull gleam of a brown iron disk and he drove over it until it lay behind the truck, then stopped.

Horns blared behind them. Macklin reached under the seat and grabbed his helmet. He looked over at Puckett, who already had on his hard hat and was looking out at the neon-lit street a little dazed. Times Square had been cleaned up in recent years, but here by the Port Authority Bus Terminal, some slime still stuck. Macklin followed his partner's gaze to a transvestite, little taller than a dwarf, who stood on the corner, staring luridly out at the traffic. He smiled.

"Welcome to nights," he said, opening his door.

They set up the area quickly, tapering out cones behind the truck with the PEOPLE WORKING sign, boxing a square safety zone around the manhole with barrier tape and stanchions, bringing out the yellow rim and the aluminum rail. Macklin took out the hooks, slid one halfway into the notch of the manhole cover and stepped up on it, levering it open. Puckett hooked in his bar, and they began heaving the iron disk onto the asphalt. To Macklin, the heavy scrape sounded the way it did the first time and every time he popped a hole, like a stone sarcophagus being breached by grave robbers in a mummy movie.

Macklin glanced at the circle of black.

"No, Indy!" Puckett said. "Don't unearth the ancient secrets!"

Macklin shook his head.

They took out the locking bar and the inner pan, put in the rim, and secured the rail. Macklin dropped the blower and light into the hole. They started up the generator in the back of the truck, and the blower kicked on, sending relatively clean air from the street through the chute into the hole. He went into the truck and put on his coveralls. There was a space heater beneath the tool bench, but it didn't do much. He'd have to call in to get it fixed before it got really cold.

He put on his gloves and stepped back out to the hole and looked down. There was a rusty ladder at the brick chimney of the hole, and he tested it with his foot before putting his weight on it. Then he grasped the rail and lowered himself into the dark.

Past the chimney, the hole opened up into a fifteen-foot-deep rectilinear chamber, not unlike a large grave. Running from end to end along both of the long walls were thickly stacked black and gray telephone cables. Macklin lowered himself between them and lifted the light. The black cables were covered in plastic, the gray ones in lead. Beneath the cable sheathing was a steel turnplate, and beneath the turnplate were the individual customer phone lines. There were a few thousand lines in each cable, maybe a hundred thousand lines running through the hole.

Macklin was a splicer, and it was his job to maintain and repair the cables, to keep the lines up and running. His gang was responsible for the Midtown Manhattan Market Area, Twenty-third to Sixty-sixth Streets, East River to the Hudson. More phone lines per square foot than anywhere else in the world. Most people thought of men on poles when they thought of telephone work, but in Manhattan, the whole plant lay underground. Macklin had been working as a telephone man almost six years now, and he'd never been up a pole in his life.

He and Puckett had been dispatched tonight to fix a damaged lead cable. Macklin spotted something halfway down the west wall, and he clambered down to examine it.

It was a lead cable that had a crack on the bell of its sleeve, the wider part of the cable where the splices were contained. By the thickness of the cable, he could tell it contained nine hundred lines. Nine hundred customers could potentially go out of service were heavy rain to fill the manhole and water to get into the wires. Some idiot who worked for one of the many new fly-by-night companies that ran fiber cable through the manholes had most likely stomped down on it but hadn't bothered to let anybody know.

The foreman had told him that he'd probably have to

rewipe the cable, an involved welding process using molten lead, but looking at it now, Macklin knew all he'd need to seal it properly was a soldering iron. He smiled in the dark. They'd be out of here in no time.

He looked up. Puckett smiled down from the world above.

"Lead cleaning tools, solder, and heat up the iron," he yelled heartily.

An hour later, Macklin emerged onto the filthy street, sweating. He dropped his hard hat to the blacktop, sat on the bumper, and drank in the cold air. He was facing the traffic, and he watched the car headlights approach and veer off to either side.

When he stood, he stopped in surprise at the area surrounding the hole. Rope tied up perfectly against the rail. Tools back in drawers. Back of the truck all neat and tidy. Puckett hovered over the tool bench busily scrubbing at it with hand cleaner and a rag.

Puckett was new, so Macklin had been a little wary. Man up top was supposed to keep an eye out for the one down below, but he'd come out of holes before to find new partners asleep. Macklin smiled as he looked at the young man's face, the determined eyes.

Things might work after all.

"Hey," Macklin said. "Lookin' good. You want something from the store?"

"Ah, sure," Puckett said, unconcealed mirth on his face. "Coke'd be great."

Macklin ducked out beneath the barrier tape like a boxer leaving the ring.

Five minutes later, he came back with a paper sack and put

it in the truck cab. He and Puckett broke down the area quickly. They put the pan and the locking bar back over the hole, and Macklin put his hook to the notch in the heavy cover and pulled, spinning it hard over the asphalt and into the hole, where it stuck with a metallic, almost musical, clatter. He took off his coveralls and threw them into the back of the truck with the cover hook and locked the door.

He stood for a moment at the back of the truck and glanced up at the office towers to the east. He checked his watch.

All the time in the world, he thought, stepping toward the cab.

They pulled over on the avenue and sat drinking their sodas.

Puckett stared out at a cluster of transvestites that stood at the corner preening, touching each other on the arm, chewing gum.

"So all these hookers are guys?" Puckett said.

"Even the ones you're sure are chicks," Macklin said. "They're guys, too."

"I don't understand," Puckett said. "Who goes for transvestites? Idiots that think they're really women? Homos?"

Macklin leaned back.

"Some idiots think they're women," he said. "And straight-up homos, I think just go for guys who look like guys. Most of your members of the transvestite fan club are seriously closeted homos, dudes who like dudes, but don't really want to admit it."

Puckett stared out. His brow wrinkled.

"That's some seriously sick shit," he said.

Macklin nodded.

"And imagine," he said with a smile, "this is only your first night."

"You've been out here awhile, huh?"

Macklin squinted up Eighth. He put down his soda and started the truck.

"Too long," he said, pulling out.

Macklin drove back to Times Square. There were still a lot of people out when he stopped before the subway station.

"You did some good work tonight. Why don't you get on home?" he said to Puckett. "I'll take care of your time sheet."

"Yeah?" Puckett said, brightening up. "What about the foreman?"

Macklin smirked. Puckett was used to working days, with a million people around all the time and three foremen breathing down your ass at every manhole. On nights, there was one foreman, who asked one simple thing of the members of his gang: get your work done. If you did, he left you completely alone. Macklin got his work done very well. He hadn't seen his boss in the field in over a year.

"You let me handle him, all right?" Macklin said. "Get lost."

"Thanks, Sean," Puckett said, beaming, and got out.

"No problem, Puck . . . What's your first name?"

"Hank," Puckett said.

"No problem, Hank." Macklin said, smiling. "And listen, get straight home now. I don't want to see you back by that bus terminal."

Puckett closed the truck's door, laughing. Macklin watched him disappear down the subway stairs. He sat for a moment. In his west coast mirror, he could see the yellow flow of the stock-ticker sign in the distance above Broadway behind him. He tore his gaze away and slapped the truck into drive.

He drove down to Sixth and made a left, staring out at the glass boxes of the office towers. He turned right onto Fifty-ninth Street and drove along Central Park and the fancy hotel fronts. He turned right again onto Fifth and started downtown, passing by the GM Building, Tiffany's, Trump Tower.

He rolled slowly. He liked this time, having finished his work, driving through the dark Midtown streets. He felt like a night guard strolling through the corridors of a museum after closing. He rolled down the window as he drove down the center of the wide avenue, letting the cold night air wash over him.

He pulled to a stop by Rockefeller Center to do the time sheets. Halfway down the block, dark flags flapped above the unlit rink, and he just sat for a moment watching them.

He had proposed to his wife, Christina, there on the ice. He'd made reservations for the Rainbow Room and was going to do it at dinner, but she'd said she wanted to skate. He remembered stumbling with her in their skates, how the snow had begun to fall through the lights of the huge tree. How he had taken her out into the middle of the rink, put his knee down to the cold, and brought out the ring. How all the skaters around had stopped to watch. How she shook in his arms as he popped the question and then whispered yes in his ear. And how all the people around them clapped and cheered as he slid on the ring.

Macklin looked away and flicked down the driver-side visor. There was a postcard of Florida taped there, and he gazed at the palm trees, the green water, the white sand. It was a picture of a town on the Gulf Coast near where he'd met his wife and where he intended to bring her back. He traced a finger across its glossy surface and flicked it back up. Then he took out a pen and started filling in the time sheets.

When he was done, he checked his watch. A little after two. He started the truck.

Show time, he thought, pulling out.

He clicked the radio back on.

". . . drove selling up sharply. Again more mergers in the news. Pharmaceutical giant NOVA . . ."

Macklin hardly listened. Past a certain point, they just replayed the same news over and over.

He drove down to Forty-sixth and turned left. He turned north onto Park, slowed, and pulled to a stop.

". . . American chemical company in the market for a biotech . . ."

Macklin clicked off the radio and looked out. There were more corporate buildings here at the boxed end of Park Avenue. He gazed at the green glass building beside him and at the affixed sign next to its revolving doors.

"CHEMTECH," it read.

Macklin scanned the street to the south and gauged the surrounding area. Then he pulled out and made a U-turn.

Perpendicular to the Chemtech building, the Helmsley Building stretched across Park Avenue like a barrier. But instead of dead-ending Park, the ornate building had two tunnels cut through its base, like those through a redwood tree. He drove the truck beneath the downtown archway and over the Park Avenue Viaduct around the MetLife Building and Grand Central Station. He exited at Fortieth Street, made a

U-turn on Park Avenue South, pulled over, and cut the engine.

Grand Central was in front of him now, and he looked up at the statue adorning its front. It was some muscular Greek with wings on his feet poised at the edge the station's majestic roof, as if to flee the immense black-glass tidal wave of the MetLife Building behind him.

For the first time that night, Macklin felt a vague, nauseous knot of something in his gut. Guilt. Fear, perhaps. He glanced at himself in the rearview mirror. He had short dirty-blond hair and blue eyes. His face was lean and sharp, smooth but for his stubbled jaw and a scar that outlined the brow bone of his left eye. The scar was short but deep and gave him a permanent squint, as if he were forever skeptical of the world and everything in it. He stared at the scar for a long moment. Then he put on his hard hat and got out of the truck.

He stepped to the back and opened the door and climbed in. From behind the generator, he retrieved a knapsack. He laid it down on the tool bench and opened it. Inside sat miniature recording equipment, miniature audiotapes, some tools, a flashlight, and some telephone equipment modified to his own design. There were some financial magazines there as well, and he slid one out and clicked on the flashlight.

He'd paper-clipped the magazine open to an article where a good-looking, dark-haired man in a pin-striped suit stood before the green glass of the skyscraper Macklin had just surveyed.

"Chemtech Embraces the Future," read the headline, and under the photograph, "Robert Brent takes the helm."

Macklin took out his notepad and opened to a page where he'd written:

Chemtech—Robert Brent
(212) 900-8009
23453, 45 x 15

These last digits were telephone company ID numbers he'd retrieved. They were the specific cable in which the CEO's phone line ran and its exact location within that cable.

Macklin closed the pad, put it in the bag, and zipped it closed. Then he strapped the bag across his back and got out.

A police car was cruising by as he was locking the truck. Macklin gave the cop a little wave, one night bird to another. The cop bleeped his siren briefly in reply.

Macklin crossed the street to where the Park Avenue Viaduct rose up from the roadway. There was a small, dark recess among the huge granite blocks, and he stepped toward it. Sometimes homeless people were curled up in the two square feet of entranceway, but tonight it was free. He took out a key. The lock was green with age, but Macklin had oiled it recently and the key turned smoothly. He opened the door, stepped in, and pulled it shut.

Inside, it was completely dark. He could hear the hollow, muffled thump of a car driving on the sloping roadway overhead. Macklin fumbled in his bag for the flashlight and turned it on. He passed the beam along the floor for rats, but there weren't any. Macklin pointed the thin beam of light toward a wide threshold that lay ten feet in to his right. He walked toward it.

Past the threshold was a short corridor that ended at a

stone wall with two metal doors in it. The one on the left was padlocked and belonged to the water department. His old partner had told him that it contained an ancient water pumping station with an abandoned access shaft sunk six hundred feet into the bedrock of Manhattan. The one on the right had a chain and a lock as well and belonged to the telephone company. Macklin took a step to the right and took out another key.

The chain slackened and rattled loose through the door when he pulled out the lock. He opened the door and stepped inside.

Years ago, the site had been proposed for a central office, but those plans had been scrapped, and now only the cables for the surrounding area remained. Just before his thirty-year retirement, Macklin's partner had shown it to him and given him the key.

"If ya need someplace to hide," he'd said, "this is it. I doubt the company even knows it's here anymore."

The chamber looked much like the manhole he'd just been in, only it was about twenty times the size. Telephone cables snaked in all directions forty feet up and down the cavernous, granite walls. They fed all the skyscrapers around Grand Central, on Lex, Park, Madison, Fifth.

The thick cables bellied down from the ceiling and hung off the walls like monstrous intestines.

Macklin stood silently in the secret vault.

Just him and half the phone lines in Midtown Manhattan.

He let the door click shut behind him.

CHAPTER FOUR

LESS THAN TEN miles northeast of Manhattan, Sean Macklin's brother, Ray, took a bite of his apple and stared out the radio car windshield into the darkened wasteland of the predawn South Bronx. Ray's partner, a twenty-one-year-old blond recruit from some Indian-sounding place in Suffolk County, Long Island— Patchogue, Ronkonkoma, Running Rabbit, Shitting Bear, something—sat beside him sleeping. Ray didn't really like the kid, so he let him snooze. Imagine, out of the Academy three fucking weeks and he'd already taken to habits that'll get you killed. Ray didn't mind instructing rookies, but they had to be willing and worthy. He wasn't gonna be Obi-Wan Kenobi to this piece of shit. Of that he was sure.

He took another bite of the apple. When he first started

the job, ten years ago, he ate traditional cop food—doughnuts and McDonald's—and washed it down with about twenty-six cups of coffee a day. He'd put on twenty pounds. At the time, he'd been working the Upper East Side herding the homeless, so it really didn't matter. When he got transferred out to Hunts Point, he'd changed his eating habits real quick. Started working out, too, for the first time since high school. He'd take any edge he could get out here in the Congo. It was a matter of discipline.

Bursts of chatter, hardly distinguishable from static, came over the radio under the dash. Ray sifted through the noise.

They were parked on a stretch of service road outside the Hunts Point wholesale food market. Every once in a while, an unmarked eighteen-wheeler, loaded to the brim with fruit, vegetables, or meat, or who the fuck knew—heroin maybe—made a left turn and pulled inside the gate. With almost the same regularity, a hooker would stroll in after it to service the trucker. Then, as Ray was unfortunately aware, the fruits of this sordid labor, as soon as quasi-humanly possible, would be transferred to one of the local drug dealers for a jumbo vile of crack. Bronx economics, Ray thought, watching a hooker shuffle in toward the market as if sucked in by the wake of the truck. Who says Wall Street makes the world go round?

The Hunts Point hooker, he mused. Bottom feeders of the very bottom itself. You could hardly slide a sheet of loose-leaf in the space between these people and the grave. The drug addiction coupled with AIDS and other diseases gave them the stunned, haunted look of the undead. If they were your dog, Ray thought, you'd shoot them. Put them out of their misery. He left those poor souls alone. It was amazing that a guy would let one attach herself to him, he thought. But then again, he wasn't some backwoods Okie truck driver up six days, cranked to the gills on methamphetamine. Maybe some scarred, toothless crackhead was better than what they were getting at home. He was from Kingsbridge. What did he know?

This fuckin' place, he thought. This fuckin' job. It was getting old. The things people here did to each other, did to their children. The crumbling buildings and streets. There had been factories here once. Industry. It'd been an Irish and Italian neighborhood then. People had left their doors unlocked. Women took evening strolls through the streets unaccompanied. Fifty years later, if there was a white face anywhere in the pale of the four-two, ten to one he was either holding, copping, or a cop. Even those die-hard geezers, whose lack of funds and genuine penchant for the miserable life made them stay in neighborhoods past their prime, had gone as the Indian tribes and dinosaurs that had preceded them, like dust into the wind.

Ray looked at his slumbering partner. Why the hell was this guy here? he thought. It was annoying. Some kid grows up on a sunny lane—backyard, split-level, leaving his bike in the driveway—and then gets on the Job and he puts on hard like he brought himself up bustin' skulls as some badass, bare-knuckle street fighter. At least Ray was fuckin' from the Bronx. At least he goddamn lived here. These pussies pissed him off. Why couldn't the punk be a cop out in Suffolk? They only made three times the fuckin' salary. Shit, why couldn't *he* be a cop out there?

He finished his apple and placed the core back in the brown bag he'd brought it in. He checked the dashboard clock: 5:07 A.M. The sun would be coming up soon enough.

Another burst of chatter came over the radio. Ray's ears perked. It was a 10-10, shots fired, not too far away. He keyed his radio.

"Twenty sixty-nine responding," Ray called out mechanically. "How many calls?"

He was asking how many people had called in about the gunfire. How legitimate it was.

"Four," the dispatcher stated.

Just what the doctor ordered, Ray thought.

"Roger," he said, dropping the car into drive.

"What's up?" his partner asked over the race of the engine.

"Nothing," Ray said. "Go back to bed."

Tires screamed as he turned a corner.

"What the fuck is up, Ray?"

"I'm bored," Ray said, hitting the siren as they ate a stop sign. "I'm just taking her for a spin."

He turned off the lights and siren as they approached the call address. They stopped in front of a ramshackle tenement that stood beside a vacant lot. It had glass in most of its windows, Ray noticed. A telltale sign of human habitation.

"Stay here," Ray said, getting out. He heard other sirens in the distance as he stepped to the front door. He smiled. The early bird, he thought.

The front door of the foyer was locked, but the glass was missing, so he just reached in and opened it. He went in to the left toward the stairs, drawing his Glock from his holster. He looked up the spiral stairwell. The third-floor landing was unlit, which was fine by him. The new blue-black uniforms they wore made him look like a fucking ninja in the dark. He turned off his radio as he started up the stairs. On the third-floor landing, he took two quiet steps and put his ear to the door of 3B. Nothing at all. He looked at the locks. Just an old piece of shit above the doorknob. He put his back to the wall across from the door and released the Glock's safety. He heard another radio car pulling to a stop in front of the building. Then he threw himself forward and kicked the lock.

He was about five foot nine, but he was squat. One-ninety, last time he stepped on the locker-room scale, not all of it on his belly either. The lock splintered out of the frame, and he stumbled in beside the door, gun raised.

"POLICE! POLICE!" he screamed.

A light came on in a room down the hall to the right. Ray trained the gun in its direction, the muscles in his jaw clenching.

"POLICE!" he yelled again. "COME OUT WITH YOUR HANDS UP!"

"*No moleste. No moleste,*" a woman's voice called out of the room. A baby began to cry.

"COME OUT OF THERE!"

A young woman in a nightgown emerged slowly, clenching the crying baby.

"*Por favor,*" she pleaded. She was close to tears. "*No moleste.*"

"Come, now," he called to her, still pointing the gun at the doorway behind her.

She walked forward uneasily.

"Sit."

He pointed to the floor in the living room past the door. "Wait here."

He went down the hall slowly, putting his finger on the trigger. He burst through the open doorway. A mattress on the floor, a pillow in a milk crate beside it. He went to the closed closet door.

"COME OUT NOW!" he commanded at the door.

He yanked it open.

Cheap-looking clothes hung on plastic hangers.

What the fuck? he thought. Who let off gunshots? The girl?

"Where's the gun?" he asked the young woman as he came back out.

She looked at him dumbly. You'd think he'd be bilingual by now, with all the contact he had with the predominantly Hispanic community, but you'd be wrong.

"*Cuando pistola?*"

She shook her head for a moment, confused. Then her eyes lit up.

"Ah, *pistola,*" she said, pointing to the ceiling.

Just then, they heard the commotion upstairs. A door being broken in and the loud crash of someone falling, followed by muffled yells.

Fuck, fuck, fuck, fuck, thought Ray. He keyed his handset.

"Dispatch? This is twenty six-nine. I need a confirm on the apartment on that shots fired on Halleck."

"Four-B," the radio crackled at him.

Fuck.

He must have been showing his emotion, because when he looked at the girl, she said, "*No moleste,*" again.

She was beautiful, he noticed. Couldn't have been more than twenty. Long blue-black hair, smooth light brown skin, gentle brown eyes. The prominence of her body through the thin nightgown didn't escape him either.

"Don't worry," he found himself saying. "I won't molest you. Um, I mean, I made a mistake." He pointed to himself, then up to the ceiling. "Mistake. Don't worry, I'll fix the door."

He fumbled for his radio, depressed it.

"Hey, Sleeping Beauty, bring up the toolbox from the trunk."

"Bring it where?"

"Just up," Ray told him.

He heard a footstep on the landing beside the open door, and he turned. Another cop. This one was short, had a mustache and bright blue eyes. Kenny O'Connor was his name. He held a brimming Adidas duffel bag in his hand. Ray looked at the bag forlornly.

"Ray," the short cop said in greeting. He examined the cracked frame. "Looks like breaking and entering to me, Ray."

"I was thinking along those same lines myself, Sarge," Ray said playing along. "How'd you guys do upstairs?"

O'Connor took a cigarette out of his breast pocket and lit it slowly with a gold lighter. It matched the gold on the watch that peeked out from the man's blue shirtsleeve.

"We arrested a suspect. An illegal firearm was found. Before arriving, my gut feeling was that it might be drug-related, but as no contraband was located . . ."

He switched the mysterious bag to his other hand, the weight of it perhaps becoming a strain.

". . . I was obviously mistaken." O'Connor switched to a more officious tone. He was the patrol supervisor, after all. "You almost done here?"

"Almost," Ray said. "Oddly enough, the victim doesn't

wish to fill out a report, but I thought I might help get the door temporarily fixed. The lateness of the hour and all."

O'Connor looked in for a prolonged beat, taking in the young woman. He smiled brightly at Ray, patting his arm approvingly.

"You see, that's what makes you such an outstanding officer of the law, Ray. Willingness to go above and beyond. I have half a mind to put you in for a commendation."

"Ah, you know me. I don't like to toot my own horn," Ray said, smiling back.

"Only more testament to your greatness, Ray." He nodded cordially to the woman and the baby. "Ma'am," he said.

O'Connor threw the bag casually over his shoulder as he departed down the hall.

After a moment, Ray's partner arrived with the toolbox.

"I saw the sarge on the stairs, Ray. He said something about shots fired?"

Ray took the toolbox.

"Get outta here. Really? I'll see you down in the car in a second, okay?"

The partner left, muttering something under his breath. Ray bent to the lock. He'd kicked the catch out from the old frame cleanly, so it was just a matter of screwing it back in. The girl went into the bedroom with the baby and came back out a moment later wearing a robe over her nightgown. He was happily aware of her closeness as she stood behind him, watching over his shoulder. When he was done, she went into the small kitchen and returned a few seconds later with a can of soda and handed it to him. He popped it open and took a sip.

"Um, *muchas gracias.*"

"*De nada,*" she said, smiling.

"I need to come back tomorrow," he said slowly, hoping it might aid in the understanding. "Fix the door better." He made screwing motions at the door. "*Mucho trabajo a puerta. Más trabajo.*"

"*Sí? Mañana?*"

"*Sí,*" Ray said. "*Mío mañana trabajo puerta.*"

She giggled.

Ray blushed despite himself. Goddamn, she was pretty.

"*Vias con dios,*" he said.

She laughed as she locked the door behind him.

On the stairs, he thought about the bag O'Connor was carrying. How much had the little fuck and his band of cronies gotten this time? he wondered. It used to be that any gelt procured on a shift was split evenly by all, but ever since Ray had gone free agent, it was a race. A run for the money.

God knew, he needed it. He owed a very bad mother-fucker thirty-six thousand dollars, and he was three weeks late with it.

He shook that out of his head for the moment and thought about the girl. Where was she from? he wondered. Central, maybe South America. How old? Eighteen, he hoped. Hell, he was only thirty-four. A little May-December action. Bilingual May-December action. He imagined the shock on his mother's face. He hadn't even gotten her name. Good goin', Ray. Real ladies' man. He thought about her apartment. The milk crate, he suddenly realized, was the baby's crib. He'd have to rectify that. It was pretty bare, he thought, but it was clean. And the way she had gotten him the soda, that was manners. A small thing, but telling. A good person.

It was funny, he thought. In an odd way, he was happy he'd kicked in the wrong door.

Outside, the sky was a bleak heather gray. He could just make out the buildings, blackened windows in the gray facades like cigarette burns in dirty cardboard. Merciless morning unbecomingly outlining the haggard skyline.

"All done?" his partner asked as Ray let himself in the car.

He stared out through the windshield.

"That'll about do it," he said as he started the engine.

CHAPTER FIVE

HE LIVES AROUND here, you know," the bartender said.

Scully rubbed at his temple and looked up from his what? Twelfth? No, thirteenth—lucky thirteenth—drink.

The bartender was gesturing at the television set on its rickety plywood shelf above the bar. A middle-aged announcer with suspiciously thick hair was talking rapidly and then a football clip was shown.

"Don 'Trivia Machine' Rogers?" Scully asked, trying to sound interested.

"Yep," the bartender said. "Frankie D. saw him walking his dog up in Foxden. He lives in that huge Spanish mission job across from the high school."

"He's gotta be rakin' it in, huh?"

"Oh, yeah," the bartender agreed. "You want another?"

"Oh, yeah," Scully said.

The bartender put a new bottle on the bar and knocked on the wood beside it.

A buyback, Scully thought. Score. He raised the bottle to the screen.

"To Don Rogers, Sports Genius!" he toasted loudly. Maybe a little too loudly, by the bartender's cold squint.

Relax, Scully told himself. Re-lax. He picked up his new beer and took a sip. Maybe he should just cut and run. Leave the bartender the eight, take the ten. Hit the all-night Korean deli on the way home for some 40 ounces. Forty ounces, he thought, shaking his head. Next, he'd be cutting a rap album. He pictured himself in the cramped room he rented at the boardinghouse, sipping from the ridiculously enormous beer bottle, wrapped in his blanket, with his black-and-white portable TV on his lap.

He picked up his cigarettes off the bar, took one out, and lit it with a match. He counted the remainder. Seven. Eighteen bucks and seven cigarettes, he thought, the extent of his vast fortune.

Un-fuckin' believable, he thought. Un-friggin' real.

He'd been a bartender recently, but the place had folded. He'd collected unemployment, but it ran out last week. He checked everyone he knew for a line on another bar gig, but he hadn't heard a thing. Maybe he could've done a broader job hunt, but with his résumé, who was he kidding? He guessed it was possible for there to be a sudden, urgent demand for a high-school-educated, washed-up ex-ballplayer and former fireman. He just didn't think it was likely.

So, he'd decided that today was the day to come up with a new plan to change his luck. He'd picked the quiet coolness of his local gin mill to inspire the creative juices, to clear out the mental cobwebs. The fact that three hours had passed and still nothing had come to him didn't discourage him.

He tilted the cold beer up to his lips for a long moment and then brought it back down to the bartop. He wiped his mouth with the back of his hand.

Something would come, he thought.

He turned toward the front door, waiting. After a minute, he rotated back toward his drink and lifted it up. It was empty when he placed it back down.

Okay then, he thought, maybe he should come up with a plan B. Plan Burger King, he thought with mortal terror. He'd passed one on the way to the bar and couldn't help seeing the We're Hiring sign in the window.

He glanced in the mirror behind the bar and held his own gaze just to see if he still could.

He had to ride it out.

He was just in a slump.

He'd been a professional athlete for christsake.

Ever since he was a little kid, his life had been baseball. He'd always excelled at it, never thought too much about it. Like the sneaker commercial said, he just did it. Ran, threw, hit. He had the tall, lean frame of a natural ballplayer, the born lanky quickness. He was recruited right out of high school and had played on a Baltimore Orioles' farm team. He remembered the day he got the call up. He remembered calling home and his dad picking up the phone.

"Yankee Stadium," he'd said, before his old man broke up, bawling like a mother on her daughter's wedding day.

Yankee Stadium, Scully thought. How incredible had that felt?

The pristine white of the bases against the rich, brown dirt. No, not dirt. It seemed more potent than mere dirt. Like soil—the rich, brown mother earth of the infield. And the grass, that wonderful, vibrant outfield grass. He'd felt like taking off his cleats and walking in it barefoot.

There he is. Tan, lank. Three days after his twentieth birthday. Stepping out of the tunnel, pausing for a moment, staring out at the crowd. The cries of "hot dogs" and "cold beer" ringing out in the sunny July air. Babe Ruth had felt it, Ted Williams, Ty Cobb. Now him.

They had started him at shortstop, and there he was, going around the horn, casually flipping each ball chest high to first base with a skull-cracking velocity. He remembered looking into the crowd during the national anthem and meeting his father's tear-filled eyes in the box seats behind third base.

Then bad things started happening.

He overthrew a double play in the first inning and a run scored. His first time up, he was still thinking about his error and he struck out on three pitches. No ball was hit to him in the next couple of innings, and he struck out again in the sixth. His second error was a dropped fly ball that loaded up the bases and on the next pitch, two more runs scored.

He was the tying run when he got up for the last time in the ninth inning. With the errors and strikeouts, he knew it was make it or break it. The first pitch was a fastball he didn't even see. The next was a curve ball that hung up a microsecond too long and he clobbered it.

He would never forget the joyous sound the ball made off the wood, like the pop of a cork out of a champagne bottle. He remembered just standing there watching it rise, a speck caught for the briefest of moments in the sodium lights, and the crowd rising and turning to follow its trajectory as it headed for the left-field bleachers. He knew it had the distance and was just about to release the built-up rush of his triumph when the ball hit the left-field foul pole and bounced left. Bounced left! Foul ball. Strike two. He didn't even see the third pitch. Strike three. You're outta there.

"Tough luck, sucker," the catcher had cackled at him, brushing past to congratulate the pitcher.

Got that one right, pal, Scully thought. Hit that nail right on the fuckin' head.

Two weeks of similar dissatisfactions and they kicked him back downstairs. Three months later, he was done with ball altogether. When he got home to the neighborhood that summer, they were giving the fire department test and he took it, passed it, and then passed the physical. But his years in the fire department were another story that he didn't like to go over at all. A bittersweet tale, only without the sweet.

When Scully glanced up from his musings, the bartender was on the phone calling a taxi. He hung up and put another beer on the bar in front of Scully.

"That's it, Scull. Drink up. Last call."

"What the fuck you talkin' about? It's twelve-thirty," Scully informed him.

"Yeah. It's also Wednesday night, and I wanna get home. Hey, I got a proposition for you. I'm gonna go around the corner for a slice. I'll give you twenty to swamp out the bathroom and the floor."

He produced a twenty from the tip jar behind him and laid it down before Scully. As if it were a given, conversation over, no assent needed.

"Mop and buckets in the ladies'," the bartender called out as he stepped out the front door.

Scully sat alone in the darkened bar.

This is what it'd come down to, hadn't it? His life. Eighteen bucks, seven cigarettes, and a mop.

Scully stood, stumbling a little. Drunker than he thought. He pocketed the twenty. He stared at the register. Wiseass hadn't done his count yet.

Should he?

He hopped behind the bar.

"Where's that mop again?" he asked the empty bar as he hit the no-sale key, popping open the drawer. He slid out five bills from the twenties' slot and closed it. He grabbed a bottle of Chivas from the top shelf.

He was coming out from behind the bar when the door opened. A bearded man in rumpled clothes walked in.

"You call a taxi?" he asked Scully.

"No, man," Scully said, passing him. "Dude in the bathroom. Be out in a second."

It was cold outside. Under the El before him, the driverless taxi idled. He thought about his long walk home. Decisions, decisions. He wandered over to the car, tried the door. Miraculously, it opened. He slid behind the wheel.

He cracked open the Chivas as he gunned down Broadway.

First dawn found him in Foxden, the next neighborhood over. Home of the haves. Fieldstone mansions presided behind landscaped hedges in the grainy light. The bottle lay empty in the driver's-side well beneath his feet. The radio, which had perhaps offended him at some point, was missing. His clothes lay strewn on the seat in the back. His beleaguered brain had latched itself onto one thought. The sports-caster. He had to speak with him. He had to know if his moment in the majors was entered in the pantheon of the man's encyclopedic knowledge. His world waited, turning on the answer.

He pulled up the circular driveway to the man's home. There was a short path to the door from the drive, which he had no wish to negotiate on foot, so he pulled the car off the driveway onto the grass. Lights went on in the upstairs window. He drove forward to the door, reached out through the window, and rang the doorbell. No answer. He tried the horn. He drove the car in a close perimeter around the base of the house peering in the windows. He was coming back around when he saw the police car pulling up the drive. He bolted immediately from the car to the private high school's playing field. His long, still muscular legs pumped. Legs that had come so close but yet so far from trotting the bags at Yankee Stadium carried him swiftly. But it had rained recently and his bare feet slipped in the mud by third base, and he went down in a sprawl, throwing up mud.

Then they had their hands on him and he was out again.

CHAPTER SIX

BRENT STOOD IMPATIENTLY in the lobby of his First Avenue building. He was waiting for the goddamn limo that would take him to the goddamn helicopter that would take him to a goddamn ludicrous Formula One race in Pennsylvania. What he really wanted to do was stay home and study the files on the El Salvadoran plant, which is what he'd done the night before, not having caught a wink of sleep. He would have canceled, but the friend who'd invited him to the event, Mitch Gabriel, was the one who'd originally recommended Guest to represent Chemtech's interests in El Salvador. Maybe he could pick his friend's brain for some insight. Until Guest called with progress, what more was there to do?

Brent was still in a state of shock. To get his hard-won

approval one second and to have it completely jeopardized the next was absurd. He'd taken considerable measures already to conceal the environmental concerns of the protesters from Allied's head, Phillips, as any hint of impropriety would send the liberal running for the hills. The cold-blooded murder of a bunch of indigenous tree huggers, Brent had a feeling, was probably something Phillips and his Greenpeace buddies would have a hard time swallowing.

Brent closed his eyes.

Guest, he prayed, call with good news.

He opened his eyes and glanced at his girlfriend, Martine, primping in the lobby mirror. Tall and dark and just turned twenty-four. Exotic, he thought absently. She was a black-haired French girl who'd been a model, but was now mainly busy being his girlfriend. She'd appeared suddenly in his life in the months following his promotion like an award. He'd bedded some good-looking women in his time living in the city, flash from upscale restaurants and clubs, acting waitresses, hot bartenders, an exotic dancer one time.

But Martine, he thought, his mood brightening slightly as he looked over at her with masculine pride, was the first undisputed piece of ass he'd ever owned.

But how fast would she be gone if it got bumpy? he thought painfully. How long was a heartbeat? He thought of her hot breath in his ear, her French curses. At least he'd have memories, he thought, closing his eyes.

Positive, he thought. Constructive thoughts only.

A black stretch town car pulled up outside. He took Martine's hand.

Mitch Gabriel smiled from around a cigar in the plush leather of the backseat. He was now the CEO of a soft drink company that was sponsoring a car in a Formula One race for the first time. But Brent had known him from their days at the Point. Mitch had been a skilled defensive lineman in college, but now most of that strong bulk had turned to fat. Though double-chinned, red-faced, and balding, money and power wafted off him like a pheromone. A striking redhead sat beside him doing her nails.

Mitch extended his hand. Brent clenched it.

Mitch turned toward Martine, giving her a courtly little bow.

"Martine, you're as lovely as ever," he said as they got in.

Martine just waved her hand at the cigar smoke and rolled down the window. Neither young woman had yet to acknowledge the other's existence. Brent and his friend exchanged a smile.

He and Mitch had been roommates briefly, but even within the egalitarian world of West Point, they were universes apart. Mitch came from a wealthy southern family with a long military tradition. Brent was the scholarship kid trying to scrape his way up. They'd bumped into each other over the years, but it wasn't until Brent had been made CEO that Mitch started inviting him to social events. Brent had thought it snobbery at first—that Mitch had finally deemed him socially worthy—but he soon learned it was more than that. They were finally compatible.

Brent looked around at the elegant interior of the car. A disheartening image came to him: He'd be on the bus heading to prison, and at the light, a limo would pull up. A tinted window would lower, and cigar smoke would billow out. Through the smoke, he would see Mitch with Martine sitting in his lap. The light would turn and Mitch and Martine would both start laughing. Tires would splash water on the bus window as the limo sped away.

"Thanks for coming, Rob," Mitch said.

"Not at all. Thanks for having us," Brent said with real effort. "What are our chances today?"

"We'll see. We've got a good driver, a so-so crew. Tobacco locks up all the talent, so it's hard. But we've got a shot. When are we gonna see a Chemtech car?"

Brent smiled. He wondered if they showed the races in prison.

"We'll have to see about that one, Mitch," he said.

"You got to take the bull by the horns there, Rob. Show them who's running that company. I bet you haven't even called back that jet broker I put you on to."

"You're right. I've been jammed up."

"That's another one of your problems. You've got to learn to delegate, my friend."

Like ordering a bunch of natives shot down in cold blood? he wanted to ask. Instead he just nodded.

"Maybe you're right," he said.

"Did he tell you about the television?" Martine asked Mitch.

"What television?" Mitch asked.

Oh, shit, Brent thought. That StockChannel thing was tonight. They wanted to interview him on the future of hard chemicals. Fuck. How could he go on about how great everything was with a smile on his face after what he'd been told yesterday? It was live, too. He'd crack. He'd have a fucking meltdown right on national TV.

"It's nothing," Brent said. "The Aspen Woods show wants to do an interview."

"Aspen Woods? The Tick Chick? How'd you get that hot pi . . ." He stopped, looking at Martine.

"I mean, that's great."

"'Tick Chick'?" Martine said, raising an eyebrow.

Brent looked over at Mitch.

"Thanks."

He turned to Martine.

"Don't worry about it," he said.

The limo took them to the far West Side. They pulled up to a fence beside the river. A cold, hard wind was blowing off the Hudson. Behind the fence was a large white helicopter, its blades beginning to spin. Mitch led them out of the limo and escorted them aboard. Inside, instead of rowed seats, there was a cabin with facing chairs and a table. When they were seated, a crewman shut the door. There was very little noise. Brent mentioned it.

"Four rotor blades instead of two for noise reduction," Mitch said. "My latest toy. I couldn't stand that tunnel traffic anymore, so if I need to get out to Newark, wham! I'm there. You like it?"

Brent leaned back in his cream-colored leather chair and peered out one of the portals as they rocked up and began to hurtle above the whitecap swells on the gray river.

"I guess she'll have to do," he said.

It took them thirty-seven minutes to get to the track in Pennsylvania. A ride that would have taken two-and-a-half hours by car. Approaching the stadium, Brent studied the crowd from the air. There were probably people from his hometown down there, Brent thought. He envisioned them smuggling in food and beers under their cheap Wal-Mart jackets to avoid paying the stadium's prices. He could picture the bullies, who'd picked on him in grammar school, sitting down to a day of high-speed fun. Men who now drove trucks long distance and made lives out of standing on assembly lines tightening bolts. Working-class, blue-collar lifers who'd probably saved up for the tickets like it was a fucking vacation. And here he was, buzzing by them, blowing off their gimme caps with his friend's ten-million-dollar helicopter.

Jesus, he thought. Jesus Christ. How could he be that ugly even in his mind?

He rubbed his eyes as the copter tilted up and came to a soft stop on the corporate helipad in the center island inside the track.

It was this fucking tension. It was ripping him apart.

Mitch's company had a trailer set up. Before it lay a catered buffet, with tables and chairs arrayed around it, under a large tent. Men in pristine white and chef hats stood behind the serving table. Mitch walked around shaking hands with his executives, introducing Brent. A skinny man with sunglasses and long hair dressed in a colorfully patched leather jumpsuit appeared.

"Rob, I want you to meet my driver, Johnny McKinney," Mitch said to Brent, presenting the thin driver.

The skinny man shook Brent's hand. His hand was small, but the grip was like a vise.

"He's the pilot of my guided missile, aren't ya, Johnny?" Mitch said. His southern accent was now cutting more sharply into his voice. "How you feeling today?"

"Oh, I feel real loose, real confident. We get our shit together in the pit today, then we're contendin'."

"That's what I like to hear. Just do your best, all right?"

"Nothin' but," the driver said. "Sir," he said, acknowledging Brent.

They got in line for the breakfast buffet.

"I gotta tell you, Rob," Mitch said. "I started doin' this for corporate promotion, but I'm really starting to enjoy it. We came in third three weeks ago down in Brazil. That's a big step for a rookie program. And that boy, McKinney, now he's backwoods, a proud, trailer-park Tennesseean, but, shit, if that fucker can't drive. Hey, take your coffee and let's go over to the tobacco tent for a second, check out the competition."

"Girls," Mitch called to Martine and the redhead, who were sitting at a table as far away as possible from each other. Neither had opted for any food.

"No scratching now. We'll be right back."

As they walked, Brent turned to his friend casually.

"Listen, I've been meaning to ask you. You know that business agent you put me on to for the El Salvadoran thing?"

Mitch looked at him silently for a beat.

"Mr. Guest?" he said.

"Yeah, Mr. Guest. Something came up, and I, well . . . How much do you trust him?"

Mitch stopped completely. He took the cigar out of his mouth. He turned and looked off into the distance.

"What came up?" he said tentatively.

"Nothing really. I'm just getting conflicting stories about something, and I wanted to hear what you thought."

Mitch paused.

"As far as I know, he's a professional. Very capable. Very discreet. Central America is a tricky place to do business, and he's represented our interests impeccably on several occasions. I don't know if I'd want him marrying my daughter or anything, but as far as business is concerned, I believe him to be a man of his word. I wouldn't have referred him if I thought any different."

"Is it true what you told me? He was in the CIA?" Brent said.

"Apparently. I've been told he was in on the Iran-Contra thing and was one of the only ones not to get burned. But who knows? How could it be confirmed? He helped you out getting that plant up and running, right?"

"He sure did."

"Then it's like my old grandpappy used to say," Mitch said, putting the same twang he had used with McKinney in his voice. "Don' look a gif' hoss in tha mouth."

Then Mitch returned the cigar to his lips, leveled his gaze forward, and began walking again. The business conference was over.

The tobacco tent was even more impressive than Mitch's. Not one person in the group was smoking.

"Hey, Jimmy," Mitch called over to one of the tobacco executives. Brent recognized him from CNBC as the conglomerate's COO. The CEO was so powerful, Brent figured, he didn't even have to come to this kind of event.

"Why don't we play for something interesting this time?" Mitch said with a smile. "How about your marketing strategy for China? I could always use a little help."

The COO studied him. He was a little man: slight, middle-aged, bespectacled. Plain enough. But the expression of icy disdain he mustered for Mitch was demonic, reptilian.

"Well, what do you . . ." Mitch started, but the executive had already turned away from him, the way one might turn away from an ant near one's foot after realizing that the debate to let it live or die was beneath one's contemplation.

"That little bastard," Mitch mumbled as they walked away. Brent's cell phone chirped. He fumbled for it.

"Hello?" Brent said. Engines were starting to gun now, and he had to raise his voice.

"Mr. Brent?" Guest said. Brent could hardly hear him. Mitch was looking at him. Brent cupped the phone.

"Sorry, Mitch. I got to take this. I'll meet you back at the tent."

Mitch nodded his head and walked off.

It was deafening bedlam by the track now, an orchestra of chainsaws. There was no way he'd be able to hear Guest. Should he tell him to call back? He spotted a row of Portosans twenty yards away. He jogged over, opened the door of one, and stepped inside.

Good God, the stench! It was quieter, though. He raised the phone to his ear.

"Yes? What happened?"

"It's covered," Guest said.

"What do you mean?"

"I've made arrangements. It's covered."

Brent rested his head against the rancid plastic wall in the dark.

Thank you, God. Thank you.

"How?" he said. "What?"

"I'll come up to share the details with you in person and bring you the paperwork. I'll be up tomorrow night. I'll be staying at the Times Square Palms," Guest said.

"How about dinner?" Brent said. Then he remembered a party he had to take Martine to. "No. Damn, I have to be somewhere. How about we get together later? I'll come to your room."

"Okay," Guest said.

"It's done, though?" Brent asked finally.

"Yes," Guest said smoothly. "You'll be pleased. Everything's been taken care of. See you tomorrow."

Guest hung up and Brent followed suit.

It's covered, he thought. What the hell was that supposed to mean? The way Guest had spoken, though, so confident, so definitive, he must've gotten the job done. Okay. Stop worrying. Even under ordinary circumstances, what Mitch had said was right. Brent didn't delegate enough. Here, he had the best in the world doing exactly what he was supposed to do. Now was the time to take Mitch's advice. An eleventh-hour crisis had been averted. He allowed himself to feel it now. Guest's assurance washed over him like a physical sensation of warmth. He stepped out of the Portosan into the fresh air and light.

Brent looked out at the crowded stands. He closed his eyes for a moment and thought of his birthplace in the mountains not far from where he now stood. He remembered the smallness, the silence, the old cars rusting in the pine-needle-covered front yards of the mobile homes.

Brent shook his head. All he'd picked up, the lessons he'd learned. Where he'd come from, where he was now. They'd taught him to be focused at the Point, to endure, to accept nothing less than success.

He smiled, looking out at the sun-dappled stands.

He had not forgotten.

He made his way back to Mitch's tent.

He and Mitch and the girls stood atop the trailer as the race began.

"This is so . . . so . . ." Martine said, her pretty little nose wrinkling as she looked out at the overweight crowd and the roaring engines.

"American," she spit out. *Ha-mare-ree-gahn.*

"Think of it as the Tour de France, Martine," Mitch said shortly. "Only with men defying death for glory instead of a bunch of frog-eating faggots riding bikes."

Brent stood under the hot sun watching the race. The cars were just screaming colored streaks. The strong smell of gasoline mixed with hot grease hovered over the smooth black roadway. On the twenty-second lap, the tobacco car went into a skid on the far turn and slammed into the wall. There was a tiny silent blur of crushed metal followed by an enormous billowing cloud of black smoke. The crowd rose in unison, craning their necks toward the scene. Brent noticed Mitch look back toward the tobacco tent. Then Mitch met Brent's gaze and smiled. Brent returned his friend's smile for a moment and then screwed his face back into a convincing expression of grave concern.

CHAPTER SEVEN

IN THE DIM room, Macklin sat watching her. His wife Christina's skin, always pale, seemed bloodless now, like porcelain. He could make out the tracings of blue veins on her closed lids. He watched her eyelids flicker, busy in dream. He bent and placed a kiss on her forehead and smoothed a hair from her face. Then he stood and walked across the carpeted floor and closed the door softly behind him.

The nurse sat in the living room reading a paperback. She was a gentle, middle-aged black woman. She put a marker in the book.

"Still napping?"

"Yeah, Rose," Macklin said. "She's doing fine. That walk you took must have tired her out. I appreciate you getting her up and out. I know it ain't easy."

The nurse shooed him with the book.

"You know us ladies, Mr. Macklin. We just gotta get out sometimes."

"How'd she do at lunch?" he said. Meals were a pain.

"She got down half a grilled cheese and some soup."

"Terrific," Macklin said. "Why don't you get out of here now. I got it from here."

"You sure?" Rose said, rising.

"Yeah," Macklin said with a smile. "You get on home."

After the nurse left, he went to the kitchen and put on some coffee. He poured some in a cup and picked it up. On the fridge, a yellowed piece of construction paper lay beneath a magnet. He passed a hand across the message Christina's kindergarten class had written there in unsteady crayon.

"Get Well Soon, Mrs. Macklin," it said.

He took his coffee outside on the front porch and stared across the road at a small field that rose to a thick stand of trees. There were farms this far away from the city. Though it was a hell of a commute to his job, he and Christina had wanted a little property, a little peace and quiet away from the world. It was evening twilight now, and the autumn trees were ablaze with golden light.

He remembered the night of the accident. They'd been out with his brother, Ray, and they were on their way home. Sean was driving. Beyond a low stone bridge there was a stalled car at a dead stop in his lane. He'd slammed on the brakes, and they skidded and hit the divider. They'd flipped over and come to a stop upside down in the opposite roadside ditch. When he turned to Christina, she wasn't there. Then he looked back and saw her lying motionless in the dark, wet grass behind the car.

She hadn't been wearing her seat belt, and she'd struck her head on the metal frame of the door. She was in surgery for eleven hours and in a coma for three days. When she came out of it, the doctors said it was a miracle.

Macklin blew on his coffee and listened to the silence of the house behind him.

Only she hadn't spoken since then, and he wasn't sure if she recognized who he was.

Dementia, the doctors called it. Irreparable brain damage. She might wake up and be fine one day or she might get worse. They didn't know. They didn't know shit about the brain, Macklin had concluded. If there wasn't something big and strange inside it, like a tumor they could cut out, you were basically shit out of luck. They recommended some hospitals to put her in, but he told them thanks, that was okay, and took her home.

It was a pain in the ass taking care of her. She needed 24/7 care, like an Alzheimer's patient or a baby. In those first difficult months, he found that it wasn't taking care of her that started to get to him, but his regular job. Every night when he went to work, it became more and more apparent that where he really belonged was home, taking care of his wife. That's where his original idea for early retirement stemmed from. It wasn't that he didn't want to work anymore. It was that he needed to work the one job that was most important.

The wind rose up suddenly, and leaves blew off the distant trees and hung in the air like golden dust.

He finished his coffee and went back into the house. He walked into the kitchen and put on dinner. When he came back into the bedroom, Christina was awake. She stared blankly, straight ahead, as usual.

"We're gonna take your shower now, honey, okay?" Macklin said.

He lifted the sheets and helped her up. He guided her into the bathroom and took off her clothes. He'd built a special bench for her to sit on so she wouldn't fall, and he slid it out and sat her down. He turned on the water and it rained down on her. She withstood this as she withstood everything—with a flat, expressionless face. He began to wash her hair.

After her shower, he dressed her, sat her at the dinner table, and went in and changed the sheets on her bed. He spoke to her at dinner while he fed her, told her about his new partner, about Florida. About how it was going to be. He sat on the bed with the TV on. After an hour, he turned to see her fast asleep. He stood, clicked off the TV and the light, and left the bedroom.

He did the dishes and put in the laundry.

The clothes were still washing when he went down into the basement. He clicked on the light. There was a workbench in the corner and, alongside it, a steel desk with a computer. He walked to the desk and sat down. Beside the desk was an old metal filing cabinet with a combination lock. He did the combo quickly and clicked it open and pulled the drawer.

He lifted out his knapsack from the night before. He zipped it open, and from among the things inside, he retrieved a small cassette tape. He held it between his thumb and fore-finger. He stared at it.

It seemed incredible to him that this little piece of plastic was capable of making his dreams come true.

But everything, he thought, seemed pretty strange since he'd begun his plan.

Overhearing the conversation of the investment banker

and the twenty-six-year-old CEO the summer before had been an epiphany for him.

How many years had he worked on phone lines and just thought of them as physical objects, thin strings of copper to be connected together or dried out? The whole time, the solution to his financial problems had been right at his fingertips, all around him in the bug-and-slop-covered cables beneath the street.

Nonpublic material. Inside stock information.

It took one conversation for him to figure it out.

Fifty-six of the Fortune 500 multinational corporations had their headquarters in his district, he had learned. Not to mention, three of the top five investment firms.

Even though listening in was illegal, and he knew it might mean his job, he decided he wanted in.

It took him two weeks to devise a listening device that he thought would work and wouldn't be discovered. He'd rigged an induction probe, one of the telephone company's basic troubleshooting tools that could monitor a line, to a voice-activated tape recorder. A week after that, stomach churning, he placed the tap on Speed's line in the middle of the night.

He knew that the only place he could hide any listening equipment was out of sight, underground, inside a cable, so he traced the investment banker's line back to the forgotten vault beneath the Park Avenue Viaduct. With possession of the banker's phone number, it was easy to find out in which cable it ran and precisely where it was within the cable.

His first tip had turned his five grand into thirty-five. Two more of Speed's mergers turned that thirty-five into a hundred. Then something happened. One of Speed's deals that he'd piggybacked had fallen through, and he'd lost thirteen thousand. That made Macklin suspicious, and when he'd gone back over his tapes carefully, he discovered a conversation that had surprised him. Speed had called an old friend of his and tipped him off about the deal.

Speed, this young phenomenon, this established Wall Street tycoon, he discovered, was doing his own insider trading. Not only that, he'd burned one of his own clients in the process.

After that, Macklin didn't give a fuck. If millionaire bigwigs were doing it, why shouldn't he? He actually needed some money. He had to be wary, though, so he'd decided to turn things up a notch. He decided to go directly to the source.

Two weeks ago, he'd overheard Speed talking to the CEO of Chemtech, an industrial-chemical company, about a merger. He learned that Chemtech's headquarters were in his district, so he'd found out the CEO's phone number and placed a tap on his line.

He fingered the tape.

Hopefully, news of the merger would be on it.

If everything looked good, Macklin would let the eighty-seven ride. Five, maybe six, more trades, he thought, and he'd be where he needed to be.

He clicked on the computer. He logged onto the Internet and brought up his trading account.

He took a small audiocassette player out of the drawer and slipped the tape in. He pressed *play.*

He recognized Speed's voice immediately in the first conversation. He turned up the volume, noting the quality of the recording with modest pride. Speed was trying to convince Brent to do a hostile takeover of Allied Genesis, the biotech they wanted to merge with, but the CEO said he just wanted a merger. The next call was Brent consulting with his lawyer.

The lawyer had just answered when Macklin heard something outside. It was a car pulling into his driveway, and he checked his watch.

Fuck, it was late. That was the night nurse. He clicked the tape off quickly and put it with the player in his pocket. He'd have to listen to the rest of it in the car on his way down to work. He clicked off the applications on the computer screen and turned it off. He tossed his knapsack back in the file drawer and slammed it shut with a bang and locked it up. Then he walked quickly across the basement, turned off the light, and jogged up the stairs to get the door.

CHAPTER EIGHT

"RAAAYMOND! RAAAYMOND!"

Ray Macklin stirred.

"Raymond!"

"WHATTT?" Ray yelled, raising his head from his pillow.

"It's three o'clock, Raymond," his mother said with a thick Irish accent. She stood in the doorway of his bedroom, small, wiry, immovable.

"Ya said ya'd drive me to the supermarket," she said.

"Jesus fuck," Ray said under his breath.

"What was that?" his mother asked.

Ray jumped up from the bed.

"I said, 'Good mornin', Ma.'"

He searched for his sweatpants. They sat folded neatly on a shelf in his closet. As he put them on, his mother began straightening his bedsheets. As long as he could remember, his whole room was kept "neat as a pin." His mother could sure get annoying, but she did keep his shit nice. He knew it was about time, now that thirty had come and gone, to maybe find a wife to look after him. The fact of the matter was, though, he was worried about his mother.

He put on his sneakers and grabbed his wallet and keys.

When she left the room, he went to his sock drawer, where he kept his Glock and his .38, along with a wide assortment of weapons he'd pocketed off perps he'd arrested over the years. Switchblades, huge foldout knives with brass-knuckle handles, belt-buckle knives, folding metal batons. He usually didn't wear his gun when he wasn't at work. Off duty was off duty, as far as he was concerned. But ever since he started owing money, he'd been arming himself pretty religiously. Better safe than sorry, especially with Ma around. He took out the Glock and put it in a belly pouch strapped to his waist. He debated whether he should bring the .38, but decided that the Glock would be enough. They'd only be out for an hour.

They left the house, a utilitarian, aluminum-sided two-family. They rented out the top half to a couple of middle-aged dykes. Old maids, his mother called them. Old maids, carpet munchers, whatever, as long as they were quiet and paid their rent on time, who gave a fuck?

Ray looked up and down the block. Nobody sitting in a parked car. Nobody hanging out on the cracked sidewalk. All clear.

They drove to the supermarket. It was a short ride, less than ten minutes away, but he always had to drive her. Like many Irish lasses who emigrated to the shores of the New World in the late fifties, his mother had never learned to drive.

He pulled into the crowded parking lot as the subway rattled by overhead on the rusted iron bed of the elevated track.

He pulled up to the front door. As she was getting out, he thought of the Spanish girl and her baby from last night's shift.

"Oh, Ma. I just remembered something. Do me a favor? Pick up some diapers."

His mother looked at him, shocked.

"Diapers! Is there somethin' ya want ta share with me?"

"Jesus, Ma. It's my partner. He told me his wife's havin' a baby. I want to get him some stuff. He's not making top pay. I thought I'd help him out."

She looked at him suspiciously as she walked away.

Ray pulled out of the parking lot and drove under the El up Broadway. He looked out the window. The old movie theater was a church now, he noticed. A neon cross had been erected above the marquee, where "Alabama Christ Baptist Denominational Christ Is Lord" was now playing. On the corner across, the front wall of an optometrist's office featured a graffiti portrait of a smiling, track-suited dude in sunglasses—a happy customer, no doubt—that had been bombed along with "SEIDENBERG OPTICS" in big, phat, Day-Glo orange spray paint. Once shopkeepers started commissioning the local vandals for advertising, Ray mused, you might as well fly a white flag from your window. The neighborhood was gone.

He stopped at a children's store, where he picked up some baby clothes. Then he drove to a Bradlees and picked up a portable crib and stroller. He rushed back to the market in time to see his mother emerge with a cart full of groceries. She glared at him again when she saw the trunk's contents.

"Ya sure everything is all right, now?" she said.

"Relax, Ma. Gimme a break."

Ray immediately noticed the man sitting in a Lincoln town car half a block down from his house when he turned the corner.

Holy shit, he thought. Here we go.

"Listen, do me a favor, Ma. I want you to go straight in the house, okay? I'll take care of the packages."

"What is it?" his mother said.

"Nothing."

He pulled into the driveway. His mother got out and went up the steps into the house. Ray followed her out, but instead of unloading the groceries, he walked alongside the house into the backyard. He climbed his back fence. He cut through his back neighbor's yard to the street behind, made a left, and ran down the block. He looked around the corner and saw the back of the man's head in the parked car. He watched him raise something to his eyes. Binoculars.

He unzipped his belly pouch.

Without taking his eyes off the man, he quickly crossed the street behind the parked car. As he approached, he could see the guy's olive complexion through the open window. Fucking guinea wants to clean my clock, does he? He took out his gun. Just as the man was lowering his binoculars, Ray stuck the barrel of his Glock into the soft part of his thick neck, just below the jaw. The man jumped.

"Hey, asshole," Ray said clearly.

"No, no, no. I'm on the job. I'm on the job. Yo, I'm a cop!"

"Oh, really?" Ray said. "That's funny. I'm a cop, too. Why you lookin' at my house, motherfucker?"

"Um, surveillance. I'm lookin' at the house on the corner."

"Surveillance, huh? Nice fuckin' ride for surveillance."

"I'm narcotics, man. Guy on the corner of your block is a coke dealer. Please, could you put the gun away? My partner is gonna be coming back any second. We don't want this to get complicated."

"No, I guess *we* don't, considering yours is the first head's gonna get a bullet in it. Show me some ID, shitbag."

The man reached into his jacket and brought out what looked like a fat billfold. Ray took it and flashed it open. A badge. A real one. Ray thought for a second, lowered his gun, and put it away.

"Detective Larry Bruno. I'm Ray Macklin. But you know that already, don't you? Because you ain't narcotics, you're a fuckin' rat. Guy who lives on the corner is eighty-seven years old, asshole. He couldn't deal a hand of poker. Somebody dropped some shit on me, huh? You sniffin' around? Well, I'd do a better job being inconspicuous, if I were you. I get nervous with people acting all suspicious, especially around my mother, you understand? Next time I might not be so clearheaded."

"My badge?" the man asked.

Ray chucked it across the street.

"Go fetch, cheese eater."

He walked back to his house without turning around. When he got to the driveway, he popped open the trunk and grabbed the packages. His mother was watching the street through the living room blinds.

"Please, Ma," he said, "don't ask."

She turned and went into the kitchen. He followed her and put the packages on the counter. Then he went to his room and lay down on the bed.

He gazed up at the ceiling.

Jesus Christ, fucking IAD. Somebody had squealed about his shift's little side trips. His partner probably. Little Long Island fuck had "rat" written all over him. What the fuck was he gonna do for money now?

How did he ever fuck himself up this bad?

He knew how.

"Raymooond!"

The heartening smell of frying steak filled his nostrils.

Thank God. A good dinner would take his mind off his troubles.

"Coming, Ma," he called as he headed into the living room and turned on the TV.

CHAPTER NINE

S CULLY HELD HIS breath. Light burning like the center of the sun through his tightly closed eyelids. The gritty, hard pillow of cement beneath his besieged head. The bitter stench of urine. The savage reverberation of steel on steel. To move, he knew, would assent to the existence of these things. He had to stay still.

He opened his eyes. Dark iron bars reached up to a scarred cement ceiling. Yep, rock bottom it is.

His mind probed gingerly into his immediate past. Bar. Drunk. Very drunk. Stolen money. Cab. Ohhhh. Stolen cab. The rest was blurry, a quick-cut montage of primordial visions. They had to be dreams, but he had the ominous feeling that they were all too real. Metal, water, trees, bushes: driving through a forest? The squish of mud between his toes. As hard as he tried, he couldn't remember a thing. That was good. No memory meant no guilt. Ignorance was bliss.

That had pretty much been his motto since he'd left the fire department two years ago.

"One goes, we all go," they used to chant when they were drunk at parties. But just one had gone, all by himself, and his name was Timmy Murphy.

It was a Wednesday morning when the call had come in. It was a warehouse fire, three blocks away from the house. They were the first ones to arrive, ideal since first on the scene fought the fire. Second company on the scene had to go in. The fire seemed to be on the fourth floor. Scully was put on the ladder and elevated to the fifth to ventilate. Murphy was new, but he was real gung ho, so he'd been put right behind him. Smoke billowed out of the first window he'd smashed out. He'd just busted in the second when he heard somebody screaming for help.

Murphy had climbed up beside him.

"There's somebody there!" Murphy had said, grabbing the sill. "Right fucking there!" Scully could remember the urgency, the anger in Murphy's words. As if the person being trapped was a personal insult to him.

Scully should have reminded him that it wasn't their duty to do it. That search-and-rescue were already in the building and they should just stay put. But he didn't. There was a vibrancy coming off Murphy that made Scully think that the kid knew what he was doing. He didn't even put out a hand to stop Murphy from swinging first one leg and then the other into the building. He remembered seeing Murphy stand there for a second, smoke blowing out over his back.

"Where are . . ." Murphy started to call out to the victim. And then he was just gone.

It'd been the window of an elevator shaft they'd busted open. The person calling had been trapped in the elevator between the fifth and sixth floors. Murphy's first step in was onto a girder. His last step had been into five stories of black, unforgiving space. They found him in the elevator pit, floating facedown in water that had pooled from their hoses.

Scully handed in his resignation the next week. He could've stayed on, he knew. Nobody ever came out and said it was his fault.

Scully rose to his knees on the foul-smelling floor.

It just was.

The cell he was in was one of four along a short hall. He was the only prisoner. It was a holding pen at the local precinct, he figured. They'd probably wanted to wait for him to sober up before they booked him. After a while, the steel door opened. A cop came into the hall and stopped before his cell.

"Afternoon," he said with mock cheer. "Let's take a ride to central booking!"

The cop cuffed Scully and took him out into the hall and through a dismal, windowless room. An overweight, mustached man wearing an ugly tie sat at a paper-covered steel desk, talking on the phone.

"This is the sports fan?" he asked the turnkey.

"Yep," Scully's ward said, peering at him as they passed. "As they were putting him in the squad car, he's yellin' up at the house, 'Let's go to the videotape, motherfucker!'"

"Did I really say that?" Scully asked the turnkey as he took him down some stairs.

"That's the least of your worries, drunko. Bar you stole from is pressing charges. Cab company's pressing charges. I heard Don Rogers is insanely angry. He thinks you were some gay stalker trying to kill him. Plus, remember, our local 'Voice of the Yankees' is a friend of the mayor's. You're getting hung is my bet."

They shuffled down past the precinct desk and out. A bright-orange-and-blue bus with wire mesh on the windows was parked at the curb. A skinny corrections guard in mirrored shades stood at the doorwell.

Scully was led onto the bus. There were three other prisoners on it already. The hunched-over shape of an old man snoozing in a seat near the front, a huge wide form of a black man sitting near the back, and a middle-aged bum, an older version of himself perhaps, in the middle. Scully weighed his options and then walked toward the old man at the front and sat across from him.

There was a cage separating the driver and the guard from the prisoners, and it shut with a bang as the bus growled to life.

"Okay," the guard announced from behind the cage, like a malevolent tour guide.

"Ya see this?" he said, holding up what looked like a flare gun. "This is eight hundred volts. Any fights, any fucking around, you're gonna get zapped. So if you don't feel like doing the jitterbug this early in the morning, or having a session of your very own personal electroshock therapy, just sit back, keep to yourself, and enjoy the ride."

It wasn't ten minutes later, after they'd gotten on the Major Deegan, when the old drunk started farting.

"Awww!" called the black guy from the back as the foul emanations reached him. He sounded pissed. "I ain't puttin' up wit' this shit. Hear me? I don't sniff *no* man's ass."

"Enough!" called the guard from the front. He took a disgusted whiff. "You people are dirty, fucking animals. They should give me a hose so I can clean you like the monkeys at the zoo. I smell that again, I'm lightin' somebody up."

The old man smiled in his drunken slumber and shifted in his seat.

The next time he farted, they were stuck in rush-hour traffic in Midtown Manhattan. If the inside of the bus had paint, it would have peeled. Then it began.

"I can't take it!" the black man yelled from the back. He stood. Veins bulged on his bald head, his huge fists clenched in agitation. "I AIN'T SNIFFIN' NO MAN'S FARTS. OPEN THESE MOTHERFUCKIN' WINDOWS!"

"SIT DOWN!" screamed the guard.

"OPEN THE WINDOWS, MOTHERFUCKER!"

"I SAID, SIT DOWN!"

"FUCK YOU!" yelled the black man, taking a step forward toward the drunk.

The guard aimed his Taser through the wire of the cage and shot.

The black man cried out as it struck him in the shoulder. First, he jittered uncontrollably, and then suddenly, he stopped. Though he was still getting zapped, it had no effect on him anymore. Scully watched a look of intense determination enter the black man's face as he turned toward the back door. He raised his huge leg. The sound of his kick was like a shotgun blast.

"AAAAAGGGGHHHHHHH!" he screamed, mule-kicking again. There was a metal crunch as the back door flew open. The black man ripped the cord from his shoulder and jumped out.

Scully glanced out the newly opened door at the flow of oblivious pedestrians on the sidewalk. He looked up at the guard, who held the impotent Taser limply in his hand, and at the drunk, who was snoring now against the window. Then Scully turned and, with a speed that was surprising even to him, kicked off his laceless, mud-caked boots and ran out into the darkening city.

CHAPTER TEN

IT WAS TEN-THIRTY when Macklin pulled into the small rest area off the West Side Highway to listen to the tape. He could've listened while he drove, but if there was any pertinent information, he wanted to be ready to write it down. He shut the engine. Beyond the metal divider, the wide Hudson spread out as dark and calm as a sheet of black silk.

He took out his little notebook. He placed the recorder on the passenger seat and hit *play.*

He listened to the conversation of Brent and his lawyer from start to finish. Brent went over their options, whether to do a merger or a hostile takeover. The lawyer told him that a merger seemed like the best idea to him. The decision was made to propose a merger at the board meeting that afternoon.

Macklin smiled.

Allied Genesis, he wrote in his notebook, *MERGER.* He underlined it twice.

There were some clicks and the next conversation started.

"We did it!!!" he heard Brent yell.

"Great news, Robert," said the lawyer. "Really great. When? Just now?"

"Just this very moment. I can't believe we pulled it off, old buddy. Thanks for all your help."

Macklin banged the steering wheel.

The merger was on.

Allied Genesis, he thought. Allied Genesis. With luck, its price would be low and he could pick up a bundle of shares. Sit back and watch it spike when the news of the merger was released to everybody else. He'd put in the order this morning.

He clapped his hands and began rubbing them briskly together.

Fucking yes, indeed.

He was about to click off the tape when he heard a different voice.

"Mr. Brent?"

Macklin stared at the tape recorder. It was another party. Not the lawyer. Not Speed.

"Mr. Guest. How can I help you?" Brent said.

There was a long silence.

"We have a problem. Are you alone?"

"Yes, I'm alone. What is it?"

"Is this line secure?"

"On this end it is. Why?"

"There's been an incident."

Macklin's eyebrows went up.

He stared out on the dark water as the two men spoke. He listened raptly to their problem, to all that was involved.

At one point, Brent told Guest to hold for a moment. Macklin listened to the caller sigh as he waited. After a moment, Guest began to whistle. Macklin recognized it right away as Frank Sinatra's "Summer Wind." His father had been a big Sinatra fan.

Guest stopped whistling as Brent came back on.

"Do whatever's necessary, Mr. Guest. Make this go away. We're right in the midst of a major merger. Two million and not a dime more. Use the account in Mexico City. And let me hear from you soon."

"I'll call you," Guest said.

Macklin absently clicked the stop button. The bulky, black plastic recorder suddenly seemed insectile, ominous, like a huge beetle in his hand. He looked out, dazed, on the water.

Thirty or forty people, he thought.

Make this go away, he thought.

When he looked into his rearview mirror, he spotted a police car. His fingers slackened suddenly, and the recorder dropped into the passenger seat. He waited for the cruiser's lights to flash and the cop to get out, but nothing happened. He turned the engine over and threw his lights back on. He rolled out over the gravel in a lawful manner and got back onto the highway. Then he stepped down on the gas as hard as he could.

CHAPTER ELEVEN

A s HE SAT in his car at the red light, Ray began to whistle. The crowd that had just burst out of the Sueuños Tavern on the corner became even more animated as the two combatants in its midst began to pummel one another. According to the patrol guide, Ray was disregarding his duty. He was supposed to wade on in there like Dirty Harry and arrest the two men for assault. The drunken, fired-up crowd wouldn't tear him apart or anything. They wouldn't make him eat his badge or beat him with his own gun. When the light turned green, Ray honked at a couple of spectators who'd stepped off the curb to get a better look at the brawling men. He looked into his rearview mirror for IAD. Write me up for that one, boys, he thought, driving away. I'll take that citation on the chin.

Ah, autumn in the Bronx, he thought, looking out the window as he drove by. Tenement after windowless tenement. Houses with windows and doors so fortified with black iron bars that the occupants appeared to be doing time. It was on the upswing, if you read the papers. Murders were down a whopping three percent. Hope springs eternal.

He was more armed now than he'd ever been. He had his Glock, of course, but he'd added the .38 to his left ankle and a switchblade to his right. He'd even put on a trick belt-buckle blade he'd taken off a skell he'd arrested a few weeks ago. Put the *u* in *security,* was his new motto.

Ray had called in sick to work that night. After dinner, he'd lain back on his bed, thinking. Maybe he needed to hide out for a little while, get IAD and Mr. Bad Dude, who was probably out looking for him, off his back. He needed some space, time to get his shit together. He had some vacation time coming, and he thought he knew a place he could chill for a while. That girl all alone in that hovel. God knew, that would be the last place they'd look for him. Besides, it'd be good to know how Ma might handle a little trial separation.

Ten minutes later, he pulled up in front of the building, parked, and put on The Club. Even old cars were stolen for gypsy cabs. He took out the stuff from the trunk and went in through the lobby. The glass was still missing from the front door. He'd get the super to work on that one. Or the landlord. There'd be a few changes made around here if he was gonna be a new tenant.

As Ray was going up the stairs, he passed a man on his way down who brushed by him roughly, almost making him drop the packages.

"Hey, watch it, asshole," Ray said.

The man stopped. He was a stocky, middle-aged Hispanic with a pockmarked face and greasy hair. He was about to say something until he met Ray's dark stare.

The man turned and kept going.

"Good idea!" Ray yelled down the stairwell after him.

When he got to the third floor, Ray walked down the hall and knocked on the girl's door. An eye appeared at the peephole.

"It's me," Ray called out. "From last night. *El policía hombre.*"

When the door opened, she was holding the baby and crying.

"What is it?" he said, entering the apartment and putting down the bags.

She started talking hysterically in rapid-fire Spanish, gesturing with her hands, bawling. *"El jefe,"* she kept saying, *"el jefe."*

"I don't understand. *No hable,*" he said. Then an idea occurred to him.

"Hold on," he said.

He went to the door.

"Lock up," he said. "I'll be right back."

He went down the stairs, left the building, and got into his car. He drove a few blocks farther south. There was a bodega on the corner, and a group of men stood in front of it, smoking. Ray stopped the car and got out. As he walked into the bodega, he locked eyes with one of the men, a roly-poly little Spanish guy with a black goatee. The man nodded. Ray went in, bought a pack of Kools, came back out, and sat in his car. A few minutes later, the group dispersed. The man who had nodded crossed the street and got into the car, looking behind him.

"Hey, Officer Ray, how you doin', man? I'd never made you in this dinosaur. You need a captain's license for this or what?"

The man's name was Tito. He was a junkie informant that Ray used from time to time.

Ray handed him the cigarettes.

"I need your help, Tito. Do a little translating for me. Only take you a coupla minutes."

"Hey, sure, man, as long as I don't know the guy."

"You don't, believe me."

Ray drove back to the girl's building and led Tito upstairs.

He knocked on the door, and the girl opened it, looking suspiciously at Tito.

"It's okay. Tell her you're just here to translate."

Tito spoke to her, stroking his goatee. "You got some good taste there, Officer Ray. A little young for you, maybe."

"Never mind that. Ask her what happened."

Tito spoke to her, and she went hysterical again. She spoke for some time. The junkie looked surprised. He asked her some questions. She answered them.

"What? What is it?" Ray asked frantically.

"Okay. This is her story. Her name's Carlita. She's from Colombia, okay? A really poor town. Her husband died or got killed or something, and she was pregnant, and she came to the U.S. to get work. The only way she could get here was some kind of agency they got down there that sets you up with papers and a job and a place to live. Only you have to work for them. When she got here, they said she had to be a hooker, but she wouldn't do it, even though they threatened to send her back to Colombia. So, they gave her another job in a sweatshop downtown. There was a lady in the building who used to watch her kid, but she moved or something, and she said she couldn't go back to work until she found somebody else."

"No way," Ray said. "Who the fuck's '*el jefe*'?"

"The boss. He's her boss. He came by just before you did and said she was fired from her job, and if she wouldn't be a prostitute, they'd take the baby."

"Get the fuck outta here."

"That's what she said. That's not all. She said he hurt her, too. Shocked her or something."

Ray looked at her. She nodded her tear-filled face up at him. She showed him her arm. There were burn marks on it.

"*Por favor,*" she said.

"Ask her what he looks like."

He did. She told him.

"Says he's got black hair and holes in his face."

"Fuck. Guy almost knocked me down as I came up. Ask her if she knows where he lives."

Tito asked. She spoke.

"Right here in the building," Tito said slowly. "He's the super."

Ray nodded grimly, slowly.

"Thanks, Tito," Ray said, staring off.

Tito left quickly, closing the door behind him.

"I'll take care of it," Ray told the girl. He walked toward the door. The baby gurgled on her lap.

"Lock up," he said.

The super's apartment was in the basement at the end of a long, dark cement corridor that reeked of piss. As he approached the door, Ray took out the Glock, made sure that the safety was off, and slid it in his jeans at the small of his back. A dog began to bark loudly from inside the apartment. A monster-sized one from the sound of it.

"Hey! Anybody in there? Hey, Super! Hello?" Ray said, knocking.

The dog was in a frenzy, scratching at the door, banging against it, rattling it in its frame. Sounded like the goddamn thing was gonna have an aneurysm.

"Hey, Super!"

An eye appeared at the peephole.

"Hey, how you doin', guy?" Ray said. "Could I talk to you about the lobby door?"

No answer. Ray heard the slick clack of the lock tumbling. He pulled the Glock. The door went ajar. Big, sharp, chomping teeth appeared in the crack. Fuckin' rottweiller.

"Hey, tie that dog up!" Ray yelled.

There was a new sound above the roaring bark. High cackling laughter. The door opened another inch then, and the beast lunged out at him on a chain. Ray jumped back. It had to be a hundred and fifty pounds, knotty neck muscles snapping beneath its dark fur, breath steam training out of its nostrils, murder in its black eyes.

Funny, huh? Ray thought, seething. He placed the barrel of the Glock between the dog's eyes and fired. There was a short, oddly quiet report, and the dog dropped and began to convulse. The spent shell ricocheted off the cement wall, rolled down the hall with a musical ting, and then stopped.

Ray jumped over the bleeding dog, yelling as he moved forward.

He slammed into the door with his shoulder. It flew back and he fell to the floor. As he was getting up, a stabbing, burning pain ripped into his shoulder. A horrible clacking sound filled his ears as he dropped his gun. Despite his agony, instinct made him fall on top of his gun, move it down toward his feet, and kick it out into the hallway behind him. The pain stopped for a second as *el jefe* dove over him, going for the gun. Ray lay there shaking. He brought his ankle up to his hand as *el jefe* grabbed for the Glock. Ray pulled out his five shot and squeezed.

A huge chunk of plaster disappeared from the wall beside *el jefe*'s head. *El jefe* dropped the Glock and froze. Ray sat wavering. His ears rang. The sharp tang of blood and sulfur was thick in the cramped hall.

Motherfucker almost got me, didn't he? he thought as fear welled up in him. Almost took him to the other side.

He got up, went over to *el jefe*, and forced him to the ground. He groped at cuffs on his belt that weren't there. He threw up loudly then, keeping the five shot in *el jefe*'s ear as he did so.

"*IIEEEEE!*" *el jefe* called out, disgusted.

Ray grabbed him by his greasy hair and held his face down in the vomit.

"What?" He wiped at his mouth. "You don't like that?"

He dragged the man inside the apartment. He held his head down and upper-cut the pistol into his face once, twice. The third time he did it, he felt something hard give—some teeth, cheekbone maybe. He groped around by the door and found the Taser the cocksucker had zapped him with. He hit him in the neck with it and depressed the trigger. *El jefe* began to jitter. Batteries flew as Ray crashed it off his head.

The man screamed and fell to his knees, holding his ruined face. He moaned unintelligibly.

Ray looked around. It wasn't even an apartment really. An

old cot was pushed up against some machinery, the boiler maybe. A filthy hot plate on an old radiator sat beside it. There was a scratched glass coffee table with *el jefe's* works on top of it: a needle, a spoon, a small bag of white powder.

El jefe began to yell. Ray went over to his bleeding form. He helped him up, dragged him over to the glass coffee table, and threw him through it.

Out in the hall, the dog lay in a lake of its own blood. He began dragging it in. Fucking thing weighed a ton. When he got it over to where *el jefe* lay, he heaved it on top of him.

"Don't you even look at that girl again," Ray said, breathing heavily, "because if I gotta come back here, ain't nothing gonna be breathing when I leave. *Comprende*, motherfucker?"

The dark eyes looked up at him. The bloodied head moved forward in a barely perceptible nod of assent.

Ray left the apartment, picked up his Glock, and closed the door behind him.

When the girl opened her door, she shrieked at the blood on Ray's shirt.

"Don't worry. It's okay. I'm all right."

"*El jefe?*" she asked warily.

"*No más,*" Ray said. "*El jefe no más.*"

CHAPTER TWELVE

MACKLIN PULLED TO a stop out in front of an old building on Forty-seventh near Eleventh Avenue. He'd called in sick to work and had been driving around. He needed to figure out what to do next. He stared up at the building's gray brick, its dark cornice, its narrow, cinder-blocked windows. Here was as good a place as any in the city to figure it out, he thought. It was where his father had been born and raised.

He recalled holidays visiting his grandparents. He could remember the steep, worn marble stairs and the stamped tin of the ceiling. The speeding trains that blew by on the lowered right-of-way out of the east window, and the ships that hooted past on the Hudson side. The family and friends packed into the tiny apartment. He could almost see his father again, laughing, with his arm around his old, skinny grandfather, see him tipping up a drink.

He loved his father. He'd taught him and Ray how to box and fish. He used to take them to Yankee games. His father had been a cop his whole life and had worked mostly in his old neighborhood, here in Hell's Kitchen. He'd been gone years now.

Macklin looked out the rearview mirror. It was dark now, and the random lights of the city behind him burned sharply against the cold night sky.

If there was one person he wished he could turn to now for advice, it was him.

He looked at the tape, still sitting on the passenger seat where he'd dropped it. From what he gathered, there were two options open to him. Somehow try to turn the tape in and expose the injustice on it, or not say a word and proceed with his early retirement plan.

So what do you think, Pop? he thought, looking up at the condemned building.

Turn it in or toss it out?

After a while, the answer began slowly to dawn on him.

He could almost see his father sitting there on the dark stoop with his arms crossed behind his head. See his bright blue eyes and his eternally skeptical grin.

You're kidding me, right? Get rid of it! he could hear him say.

Make your money.

If you don't look out for yourself and your own, nobody will.

Macklin sat there. He finally nodded.

That's what he'd been leaning toward. It was a fucked-up

atrocity, what was on that tape, but he had his own problems. He was burnt out, working all night and getting a couple of hours sleep and taking care of his wife. The fact of the matter was that he needed drastic financial rectification in order to get his life back to being tolerable again.

He'd go on with his plan and forget he heard the last part of the tape, he decided.

He'd just invest in Allied and make his money.

Some dead people a million miles away was sad, he thought, starting the car. But it had nothing to do with him.

He drove up to Broadway. There was an all-night deli there on the corner, and he parked at an empty meter and got out. He bought a cup of coffee and brought it with him to one of the little plastic tables at the back. He sat drinking it. There was a silent TV playing in the corner, and he looked up at it. Some business channel, couple of double stock tickers flowing by beneath a man and a woman in suits.

See, he thought, even in this dinky-ass Korean deli, they had an eye on the stock market. Everybody was making money. Fuck if he wasn't gonna make some, too.

He was sipping coffee when the name appeared below the man on the screen. His hand shook and the coffee burned his chin as he read it.

No.

It couldn't be.

"ROBERT BRENT," it said.

Son of a bitch, he thought.

He walked over beneath the TV, stood on a chair, and turned the volume up.

"Well, Aspen, the chemical industry is going through a real transformation right now," Brent was saying with a smile.

His teeth were white and straight. He paused and looked up as if reflecting on which thought to pull down from the air above his head.

"I liken what will soon go on in our industry to what happened to the telephone companies a decade ago. A shift from a static, old-fashioned, industrial business mode, if you will, to a more dynamic, consumer-oriented model."

The camera switched to the host, a waifish, Waspish young blond woman.

"A shift to where? Pharmaceuticals? The health industry? Biotech?"

"Those and others. I think we in hard chemicals see the emerging technology as an opportunity to broaden our paradigm. To create more of a chemistry company than a chemical one. We're concerned with, I think, what most Americans are concerned with today: technology, concerns about the environment, and ways to help people live more healthy, fulfilling lives."

Macklin's mouth opened. He looked in awe at the screen.

"You fucking cocksucker," he said.

"Well, terrific," Aspen said, puppy-dog innocence in her big blue eyes. "I'm sure a lot of people out there would be happy to hear such a positive approach from a chemical head."

"Well, it has to start somewhere," Brent said solemnly. "If not here, where?"

The camera cut back to Aspen, still looking admiringly at Brent.

"We'll be right back," she said.

Macklin stepped back down, dazed.

The lies!

He sat back down at the table.

That smiling prick, he thought. "To help people live more healthy lives." After he's in on a fucking massacre!

Macklin heard a clatter to his left and looked back toward the deli's kitchen. Through the doorway, he could see a small brown man bent over a steam-filled sink, scrubbing a pot. He pictured him making his way home warily through some war zone neighborhood, the smiling brown faces of his kids as he stepped into his cramped apartment. Worked hard, got paid nothing, and considered himself lucky. Probably sent money back home.

Macklin shook his head, picturing Brent again sitting back all trim and sharp in his pin-striped suit. That big fucking smile on his face.

Cool motherfucker thought he was home free, didn't he?

No, Macklin thought. He didn't think it. He *knew* it.

Screw it, he decided.

Fuck him.

How could he ever look at himself in the mirror again if he did nothing? He needed money, but there had to be less flat-out evil ways to make it. Mugging old ladies, for example.

No, he thought, he had to turn the tape in.

Macklin squinted up at the set as the commercials ended. Brent appeared again. The blond woman asked him another question, but when he started to answer, all Macklin could hear him say was, "Make this go away."

Macklin stood. He looked into Brent's confident gray eyes.

"In your dreams, motherfucker," he said.

He walked out to his car and got in. He'd just have to make some other moves. It would be harder and take longer, of course, but what else was new. There were new deals cut every day.

But he'd have to turn the tape in anonymously somehow, because if it got back to him, he was fucked. He thought of his brother, Ray. Ray was a cop. He knew lots of people: prosecutors, reporters. He'd know what to do.

Macklin took out his cell phone.

He laughed for the first time that night as he thought of his brother.

Ray was gonna flat out shit when he heard this.

He looked at the stock ticker down the block. He could almost see his father standing beneath it twirling his billy club. Disappointment in his face.

Don't be stupid, Seany, he could hear him warning him. Make it now.

"Sorry, Pop," he said, dialing his brother.

"Not this time," he said.

CHAPTER THIRTEEN

AY ROLLED OVER on the plastic-covered couch and stared up at the ceiling. A car drove by somewhere outside with its radio on, amplified thumps of bass like a distant mortar attack. He could picture the driver. Some sleepy-eyed drug dealer, all of sixteen, Yankee cap cocked at an angle so arrogant you couldn't help but itch to knock it back straight with a hard right, guiding a low-ride Honda Civic with lots of chrome flash and his tag, El Gato or some bullshit, across the top of the tinted windshield in gold calligraphy. He shook his head.

"Howdy, neighbor," he said in the dark.

He kept an ear to the outside hall. A part of him hoped *el jefe* would come on up. Man wanted to die, then he'd be more than happy to oblige him.

Carlita had been ecstatic at the turn of events. Ray had put the crib together. When he was done, she got the baby and put him in it.

"He's a cute little guy, isn't he?" he'd said, peering over at the sleeping child. "Lucky kid, got your looks."

"Listen," he'd said. "Do you think I could stay here? No funny stuff or nothing. I need a place to crash for a little while."

She'd looked at him.

He'd pointed to himself and then at the couch.

"Me stay."

She smiled.

"*Sí, sí.* You good man," she said. "*Ray es un hombre bueno.*"

Yeah, Ray thought, putting his hands behind his head. He was a good man all right. Real top fucking drawer.

Now, if only he were a good gambler.

But he wasn't, he knew. He was a degenerate. The kind that not only doesn't know when to fold 'em and walk away, like wise ol' Kenny Rogers liked to croon about, but that habitually refuses to acknowledge when he's in over his head. The kind who's perpetually sure he will dominate, especially in the face of overwhelming facts to the contrary. That all the losses sustained so far are only to heighten the drama of the certain final victory that will even the odds plus a million.

A true sucker. A fucking sucker's sucker, when you came right down to it. Even now, with this fucking guy after him, looking to what? Break his legs? Kill him? He still longed to go back down there, among the bright lights, the clanging bells, the constant hint of promise.

The thirty-six large had seemed like such a godsend, too. Manna from the Lord on high.

Ray and his partner had gotten a call about a bad smell emanating from the apartment of an old man in one of the precinct's northern tenements. They went to check it out and found the deceased, a skinny old bastard who, it seemed, had slipped and cut open his head while trying to take a bath in an intoxicated state. The overturned scotch bottle in the black lake of blood beside the toilet being the telltale clue. The guy had been dead maybe a week, and the stink was enough to drive Ray's greenhorn partner out to the hall for some air. While his partner was pulling himself together, Ray proceeded to toss the dead man's bedroom. There, under the unmade bed, was a paper sack. He'd assumed it was a month-old bologna sandwich, or something equally vile, until he opened it up. Stacks of brand-new Benjamin Franklins stared up at him. Three hundred and sixty of them to be exact. If he'd had any curiosity at that time as to how so much green had found its way to such an unlikely local, he'd postponed it. He was otherwise occupied stuffing the bills beneath his bulletproof vest.

They'd identified the body from the man's wallet on the dresser as that of one Carlo Martini. When they identified his next of kin as a son, Rocco, who held an address on Arthur Avenue, an infamous Mob enclave, it occurred to Ray where the money might have originated. But it didn't deter him from keeping it. Nor did it keep him from losing it all the next weekend in Atlantic City.

It had felt pretty bad, getting epically trimmed like that. He'd gone down in a limo and had his bag sent up to his room while he went to the craps table. Forty hours later, the bellhop went back up and brought it back to him unpacked. He felt even worse Monday morning when he received a phone call from

Rocco, son of the deceased. He wanted his "fucking money back" or he was going to blow up Ray's "fucking house." Protestations by Ray to the contrary had been to no avail.

"What? You don't think I got contacts, you fucking scavenger? You fucking grave-robbing piece of shit. I hear you're one bad fucking gambler," Rocco had told him. "And don't think being a cop changes a fucking thing. Two weeks you got to pay me back, otherwise you better make sure your life insurance policy is in order."

That had been three weeks ago. He'd put off most of what Rocco said as idle bullshit, but had been on a vague search for the cash anyway. A week ago, he'd gotten an odd phone call that had changed his attitude. An Italian friend, his first partner out of the Academy, called him out of the blue. This friend had gotten canned a couple of years earlier for illegally discharging his weapon off duty. That he had discharged it in the direction of some Washington Heights drug dealers at four o'clock in the morning hadn't made the papers, but it had gotten him fired. He'd called Ray up, said hi, and casually asked if Ray owed anybody any money.

"Yeah, well, kinda. I guess," he'd replied.

"Well, you might wanna think about paying those people back," his friend had said.

"Yeah?"

"Ah, yeah."

"Appreciate it," Ray had said.

"Don't mention it," said his old friend. "To anybody."

So that's why he'd been so cautious with the IAD detective. That's why he was acting so paranoid and desperate.

The goddamned detective. As if he didn't have enough to worry about. What if they'd been watching him for a while?

What if they already had shit on him? He saw himself in an orange prison jumpsuit walking into the cafeteria on Rikers. A cop? Forget it. He'd been to the Bing. He could fight, but if he were fucking Bruce Lee, those maniacs would still get him down, pull a train on him.

Oh, he was a good man all right, he thought.

Good at fucking himself up royally.

His cell phone began to trill.

He was gonna let it ring, but then thought about his mother. He picked it up.

"Yeah?" he asked.

"Hey, what's up, asshole?" the caller said. Not Ma, not a guinea voice either. More sarcastic, familiar.

"Sean?" Ray asked.

"No shit, Sherlock. How ya been?"

"Hangin' in there, motherfucker," Ray said.

"Listen, I was wondering if we could hook up. I got a little problem I was hoping you could help me with."

He's got a problem, Ray thought. We all got problems, he felt like telling him.

"When?"

"How about tomorrow? Earlier the better."

"Okay," Ray said. "How about the diner at ten? I'll let you buy me breakfast."

"See you tomorrow."

"Later," Ray said, hanging up. IAD, *el jefe,* now a call from his brother. This week was getting weird.

CHAPTER FOURTEEN

IT WAS A quarter to ten in the morning when Macklin pulled into the parking lot of the Van Cortlandt Diner. He shut the ignition and looked out at his old neighborhood. The crumbling tenements up the hill behind the rusted elevated track were almost white in the morning light. Above the grease stench from the diner, he could smell the sugar from the industrial bakery by the highway. A train crashed into the station above with a deafening rhythmic clatter. At least some things didn't change, he thought. He opened the door and got out.

He walked into the restaurant and looked around. Ray hadn't arrived yet. He took a booth by the window. The waiter came over, and he ordered coffee. He was on his second cup when a huge Buick pulled into the lot and parked. The dented door opened and his brother emerged.

Ray wasn't tall, but he was broad-shouldered. His head was shaved almost completely bald.

Ray walked in and sat across from him. The resemblance between them was subtle. Sean was tall, lean, and fair like their father. Ray was shorter, stocky, darker, like their mother's side of the family. But there was something, in the shape of the eyes maybe, the set of the jaw, that showed them to be related.

"Hey, Ray. Thanks for coming," Sean said. "You on your way to work?"

"Off till Friday," Ray said.

"You on days now?"

"Splits."

"That sucks."

"Tell me about it," Ray said. "Nights for you still, right?"

"Um-hum."

The waiter came over and took their orders. Ray got pancakes. Sean just ordered more coffee. Ray looked at him when the waiter left.

"So, Sean," he said, "spit it out. Call in the middle of the night. Mysterious breakfast meeting. The suspense is fucking killing me."

Sean looked out at the bright street.

"I, ah, got a little situation," he said.

"Concerning who? You? What? Legal trouble?"

"No, the other kind," Sean said, looking back. He lowered his voice. "Illegal trouble."

His brother looked surprised.

"What?"

Sean took out a tape player and headphones.

"What's this? You join a garage band?" Ray said.

Sean shook his head slowly.

"What's on this, if it comes back that you knew about it and you didn't do anything, you could get in trouble."

Ray smirked.

"What's up, Sean? You transfer from Ma Bell into the CIA? Is this tape gonna self-destruct or somethin'? What could you possibly tell me that could get me in trouble?"

"The lines downtown," Sean said. "I've been playin' with the phone lines."

Ray looked completely baffled.

"What do you mean, playin' with them?"

"I've been listening in," Sean said. "I've been tapping into them for a few months."

Ray looked over his shoulder and back quickly.

"Tapping in? Listening? What do you mean? Like for jollies?" Ray asked.

Sean laughed, relieved. His confession was like a weight off his shoulders.

"No, Ray." He leaned forward. He was almost whispering now. "For stock info. I put a tap on an investment guy who does mergers. I find out what companies are about to be taken over or merge, and I invest in them."

Ray looked at him wide-eyed, a smile played on his lips. Pride.

"Insider trading?" he said. "You bastard, why didn't you let me in on it? You make any money?"

"A few bucks. I want to take Christina back down to Florida, get her the fuck out of here. Only now there's a problem."

"Somebody's on to you?"

"No," Sean said solemnly. "I heard something that ain't good, really ain't good."

He pushed the Walkman over to his brother.

"Take a listen," he said.

Ray put on the headphones and hit *play.* His eyes narrowed in concentration as he listened. After two minutes, he hit the stop button.

"Is that for real? I mean, is that for fucking real?"

Sean nodded.

"'Summer Wind,'" Ray said. "Sinatra fan, huh? That's nice."

"You know the guy giving orders there? Brent?" Sean said. "He's the head of a chemical company, Chemtech. Ever hear of it?"

"Maybe," Ray said. "I don't know."

"You will," Sean said. "That merger he's talkin' about is gonna make his company gigantic. That's why he's trying to cover things up. One whiff of that incident will send the other company running."

"Right," Ray said slowly. "And . . ."

"Well, I think the cocksuckers should be held accountable for what they did. The company they're merging with is a biotech. They make drugs and shit. Is he gonna be paying off the FDA to pass bad drugs? I mean, what's next? You heard him."

"Isn't that gonna put a crimp in your early retirement plan?" Ray said. "I thought you said you invest in companies that are gonna be taken over. This incident comes out, there ain't gonna be no deal."

"Other fish in the sea, Ray. I'll get the next one that comes along, or I should say, we will, if you want in."

Ray smiled.

"Free money? Fuck yes, I want in. What do you want me to do?"

"Hand this tape in to the NYPD, the FBI, Immigration, whoever. You still know that guy who works at CBS?"

"Yeah."

"You fucking send it to him, too. We blindside Brent, with indictments and lawsuits and bad press. Watch the fucker burn."

"But why bother?" Ray said, leaning across the table and opening his palms. "If it wrecks the deal like you said, it's gonna fuck us, too. Let's just make our money and forget it."

Sean looked into his coffee cup. How could he explain it? What was it about? The contrite look on the fucker's face? His conscience?

"I know, Ray, I know. But I can't. It's . . . I just can't, okay? It's just the way it is. I gotta turn it in."

"You're crazy."

"I know. You're right. Will you do it?"

"You got other pigeons lined up?"

Sean smiled.

"You sure you're a cop?" he said.

"Fuck you. Are you sure you're a phone guy? Tapping into the lines you're supposed to fix? I'm gonna write fucking letters from now on."

"Does that mean you'll do it?"

"Yeah, I guess. Only what happens when the FBI asks where I got the tape?" Ray said.

"Gimme a break. You tellin' me you don't know anybody? You can't come up with something?"

Ray squinted.

"Yeah, maybe," he said. He grinned. "When the hell did you go Wall Street anyway?"

"The Internet, Ray. Ever hear of it? You know those plastic boxes with the typewriters in front of them? They're not TVs."

Ray scowled at him and raised a fist.

"If you weren't about to make me some money, I'd kick your skinny ass right here. Speaking of which, my wallet's a little thin these days. I don't know how much I could toss in the kitty."

"I got you covered," Sean said. He smiled again. "Sounds to me like you're in, Officer."

"Yeah, I guess I am."

From across the table, Sean clapped his brother on his shoulder.

"I knew you wouldn't let me down," he said seriously.

The waiter brought Ray's pancakes and left.

Sean stood. He left the tape player on the table.

"I gotta split and let the nurse off. You take that, okay? See what you can do and give me a call in a few days, all right? In the meantime, I'll get rid of my bug."

"'My bug,'" Ray said, shaking his head. "My little brother, the fucking puppet master of Midtown."

Sean put a finger to his lips as he walked away.

SEAN SAT FOR a moment in his car in the parking lot. To this point, he'd felt complicit, but now that the tape was out of his hands, he felt lighter, cleaner. Plus, it was gratifying finally to let someone in on his secret. He'd been sitting on it for almost six months and it was giving him an ulcer.

He glanced back to the diner window where Ray was hunched, working on his pancakes. He smiled. He was glad his brother was involved now. It'd been years since they'd done anything together, and maybe this could work out for him, too.

In the diner window, Ray looked up. He put a finger to the side of his nose in a secretive gesture and smiled.

Sean laughed as he started the engine.

He knew his big brother wouldn't let him down.

CHAPTER FIFTEEN

RAY SAT AT a bar across the street from the diner.
His brother, he thought. His little brother,
pulling a world-class swindle in the city. Listening
in on CEOs? Shit, he'd never heard of such a thing. He always
knew Seany was nuts, of course. He'd just thought that when
he'd come back from Florida and got married, he'd calmed
down. Once you had balls in your pants, Ray figured, finish-
ing his beer and gesturing to the old barman for another, you
always had 'em. Even if you didn't use 'em for a while.

He took out the tape and looked at it. Cold shit. Guy's
company fucks all those people and he says sweep it. If they
were able to put this tape in the right hands, this guy, Brent,
was going down.

Ray took a long sip of his beer. Maybe he'd get a commendation. On second thought, no he wouldn't. The whole deal would have to be hush-hush or he'd have to explain where he got a hold of a phone-tap recording. Even if he could get some credit for it, how would that help him? It wasn't like Rocco wouldn't still be after him for his money or IAD would be off his ass.

Jesus Christ! Internal Affairs! That's all they'd have to hear, that he'd obtained some illegal phone tap. No, there was a problem here, he thought. Turning the tape in was going to be a problem.

The itch of an idea started in the back of his mind. He took another sip. What if, instead of turning in the tape, he went to Brent with it and offered to sell it back to him? Shake his ass down. Fuckin' guy was pretty eager to empty the piggy bank to haul his shit out of trouble down in jungleland. What was a little more to smooth things over up here?

Nah, he couldn't do that. Seany had been pretty dead set about doing the right thing here. Sean had only let him in on the deal because he'd agreed to turn it in.

But what if he shook the guy down first and then turned it in? That would be fucking beautiful. Burn the jerkoff twice. Ray could pay Rocco back with interest, and then he'd have some money left over to toss on other stocks his brother came up with.

That was it.

That was the plan.

Ray glanced at himself in the mirror behind the bar, then quickly looked away. Took a real straight arrow like him to catch the angle on this one this quick, didn't it? On his own brother, too. Make a play on his own flesh and blood. He shook his head and took another sip of his beer. Fuck it, he thought. He was sinking fast. He didn't have the luxury of choice. Plus, he thought, putting the tape securely inside his coat pocket, he'd eventually do what his brother had asked him to do.

Some rich guy like that gotta be shitting his pants staring at some prison time, even white-collar, country-club time, Ray thought. Guy who's willing to buy his way out of taking responsibility for a few dozen bodies because it'll drop the fucking company stock. Who knows what he'd be willing to do with some cuffs slapped on him? Whip out his checkbook in record time if he thought it could keep him out of the clink was Ray's bet.

He'd seen it before. More times than he could count. Throw a crack dealer up against the wall and tell him, That's it, you're takin' a fall; and then time how quick he'd come out with a wad of dirty twenties, begging you to take it. And crack dealers were a hell of a lot poorer and a hell of a lot better equipped to do time than some rich, soft fuck.

It was human instinct. Man has his priorities. Jail was worse than losing money. Something from high school had always stuck in his mind, probably the only thing. It had been said by his biology teacher, a small, bony guy with a superlong filament of hair stretched to the breaking point across his huge expanse of bumpy skull. One time, Ray had come out of his daze to hear the man talk. Animals have their priorities, he'd said. Take a frog for instance, a simple frog, and place him in a tight, dry, confined area. At first, he'll jump, agitated at this new, undesirable living space. Now, starve this frog, deny him sustenance, and soon his agitation subsides as a new, stronger impulse—hunger—takes over. Then, put an airtight bell over this frog, and his desire for oxygen quickly supercedes that for food. Finally, set him on fire and his final desire is not for food or air, but for extinguishment.

Now, why anybody would want to fuck a frog up that bad, Ray didn't completely understand. But he thought he could grasp the lesson the sick egghead was trying to impart.

He'd seen and used that lesson firsthand on the street.

When he'd initially gotten transferred from Manhattan to the Bronx, he worked days and everything was fine. He did his job, which was a hell of a lot busier and more exciting than it had been on the Upper East Side. It was only when he started working nights that he began to get involved in crazy shit.

His first night partner was Kenny O'Connor. One night, they were performing a routine traffic stop. Ray was driving, and an Oldsmobile had failed to signal as it turned onto a side street. Kenny had told him to pull the guy over. Ray remembered thinking, Jeez, this guy's a stickler. Kenny told him to wait in the car, and when he got back in, he was carrying a shoe box.

"Drive to the Yard," he had told him.

Ray drove. The Yard, a favorite cooping spot, was an abandoned parking lot between the old Oak Point freight yards and the sewage treatment plant on the East River. On the dark water, you could see the prison lights on Rikers. Ray remembered looking at those lights and then at the shoe box.

Kenny popped the lid off the box and spilled the bundle of rubber-banded, soiled green on the front seat of the cruiser.

"Here's the deal," Kenny had said. "You got a decision to make here. You say yes, you get half this score and you're in. You say no, I make this disappear and we get you a new partner. I gotta tell you, though, you say no, you better go back on days because you're gonna be isolated, all right? What's goin' on here's fucked up. I know it is. I'm doin' it anyway. They don't pay me enough to risk my neck for this bullshit. What's it gonna be?"

"Count it out," he'd said after a moment. Had he even thought about it? The money was there. They were the cops. It was no choice at all.

After that, it was just routine. You came across a drug dealer; you shook him down. Shots-fired calls were the best. Not only because of the adrenaline rush of action, but because of the promise of reward. He'd been gambling before he started making money, and the windfall of cash just helped him lose bigger.

So, he knew a couple of things about the squeeze play. Working on the Upper East Side, he had had the unfortunate occasion to come across people like Brent. They'd get a call about some prowler at a brownstone off Fifth or Park. It'd turn out to be some bum, camped out for the night. They'd roll up on him and move him along. If he was unconscious, they'd call a bus. Let the EMS guys earn their paycheck, put their gloves on, scoop his ass up, and take him to a hospital or a shelter. Even if the rich prick who'd called in the complaint had the wherewithal to say thanks for taking out the trash, he wouldn't do it himself. He'd send the maid out to do it.

Yeah, he knew how to play it. He'd need a partner, though.

He sat and had another drink. After a while, the front door opened and a clean-cut black guy walked in. He went over to the bartender and showed him a sheet of paper. Bartender shrugged his shoulders and shook his head. What's this? Ray thought. More IAD bullshit? The black guy approached him next. Ray flashed his badge.

"What's up?" he asked.

"You see this guy?" the black cop asked, showing him the

sheet. Holy shit! It was a photograph of a friend of his, Jimmy Scully. The Scullboy.

Ray studied it for a long moment, then shook his head.

"Nope," Ray said. "What'd he do?"

"Escaped from custody. Lives around here. Thought he might head back," the cop said.

"What was he arrested for?"

"Hit and run, grand theft auto, trespassing, drunk driving. Whole bunch a shit."

"How'd he escape?"

"On the bus transport to central booking, another prisoner went berserk and kicked open the back door and ran. We caught him. This boy here decided to haul ass as well."

"When this happen?" Ray asked.

"Yesterday."

"Hey, I see him, I'll call it in."

"Thanks a lot, guy. Check you later."

The cop left.

Scully, Ray thought. Local boy done good, done horrible. Played ball for a split second with the Orioles. Whole neighborhood went over to the stadium to watch him choke. Fireman for a while. Now, he's a felon and fugitive from justice. My, how the mighty have fallen. Poor fucking sap. He could empathize. Scullboy's luck seemed about as good as his own. Maybe it was the neighborhood, electromagnetic field from the El or something.

Ray was polishing off his fourth breakfast drink when the door flew open again. A tall figure filled the doorway. Unshaven, unkempt, filthy sweatshirt, dirtier jeans, standing there in some old, rank sneakers. Ray recognized the face behind the dirt immediately.

"Hey, Scullboy," Ray called out loudly with a wide smile.

Ask and you shall receive, sayeth the Lord, he thought.

"Get your ass down here and let your old friend buy you a beer."

"A BEER?" SCULLY said as he approached his old friend, Ray Macklin.

"Now, why didn't I think of that?"

As he sat, Scully looked at Ray's big, friendly smile. Not good. Ray was an old friend, a generally good guy. Take care of a ticket for you. Buy you a drink. Slap you on the back. Lately though, Scully didn't trust him. Ray had been a regular in the bar where Scully used to tend. He'd seen the gambling, the mysteriously fat bankrolls no cop had any right to possess.

Old friend or no old friend, Ray was into some funky shit.

"Hey, long time, no see, Jimmy. Why don't we go to a table in the back, little more private."

Scully squinted at him.

"Okay."

Scully leaned around to the bartender.

"Let me get a double shot of Jack and a Bud."

The bartender didn't move. He directed his heavy, worried gaze toward Ray. Ray nodded.

"It's okay, John. We'll go in the back, all right?"

They walked past the pool table and the bathroom doors and went out the fire exit into a tiny, square courtyard. Budweiser boxes were stacked up a wall. The morning sun illuminated the cement. Ray kicked a crate over to Scully.

"Little bright here, don't you think?" Scully said as he sat. He knocked back the Jack, and then sucked at the beer until it was half gone.

"Fuck, I needed that," he said.

"Jimmy," Ray said, looking at him. "What's goin' on with you?"

Scully listened to the subway blow by in the distance, a rattling clank like the chain of a ship pulling anchor.

"I'm a popular guy, huh? People comin' around askin' about me?"

"See!" Ray said, throwing his hands up in the air and looking skyward. "I don't get it. You're a bright guy, talented. How do you manage to fuck yourself up so bad?"

Scully smiled.

"You gonna counsel me, Ray? Is that what you're gonna do? Because if that's the case, slap the cuffs on me right now. Otherwise, honestly, you can shove that shit up your ass. I've had a bad enough couple of days as it is."

"That's right," Ray said. "You've had it pretty rough, with all that car stealing and running people down, and escaping from jail and shit. You must be ready for a fucking vacation. Cop came in here twenty minutes ago with your picture and said he wants to make sure that you get it. I wouldn't be spurnin' any advice at this point, if I was you. Looks like you could use a friend."

Scully looked amused.

"Oh, is that what we are? Friends? Listen, Ray, save that shit for the broads."

"I guess you want me to call up that cop, like I told him I would. You know what could happen to me I get caught talkin' to you? You know what 'aiding and abetting' is?"

"Nope," Scully said. "But I know you, Ray. What's the angle?"

"Okay, smart-ass," Ray said, pointing a finger at him. "Angle's this. I could burn your ass. I'm obligated to. But I'm not gonna. What I am gonna do is offer you a place to stay until it ain't so hot for you anymore."

"For?"

"Now that you mention it, I got a little job you might be interested in. But here ain't the place to talk about it. My car's out front. Why don't we take a ride?"

Ray went out first to his car parked across the street. He unlocked the back door and then looked up and down the block, but didn't see anyone. Just his luck to be pulling this shit a day after learning there was an IAD tail on him. Since he hadn't been at his house yesterday, he'd probably lost them. He whipped a U-turn and leaned on the horn. Scully came out, opened the back door, and lay down on the floor.

"When was the last time you cleaned up back here?" Scully asked.

"While ago. I cleaned up the trunk yesterday, though."

"Here's fine," Scully reconsidered. "So, what's the job?"

"Plenty of time for that."

Half an hour later, Ray stopped and cut the engine.

When Scully sat up and looked around, fear shot through him. They were on a block that had as many empty lots as residences. The tall, brown shrubs among the rubble and garbage in the lots indicated that they'd been that way for years. It looked as if trees would soon start growing and animals would return: rabbits, deer, bears. They were parked in front of a building that was missing windows, not just the glass, but the actual window frames.

Ray led him into the building and up some old stairs to an apartment on the third floor. Ray opened the door with a key and walked in. Scully didn't know what he expected to see, but it definitely wasn't the pretty Spanish girl and the baby who were sitting in front of the TV in the living room. *Barney* was on and the baby was clapping its pudgy little hands.

Ray went into the kitchen and came back out with two cans of Bud.

"Scull, this here's Carlita and her baby. And let me point out, not my baby, but hers and hers alone. Carlita, this here *es mi compadre*, Scull. If he touches you, let me know. I'll shoot him."

Carlita waved, smiled.

"You know any Spanish, Scull?" Ray asked.

"*Cerveza*'s about it."

"Well, that kinda sucks, because she *no hable* word one of *Inglés.*"

They sat at a little table in the kitchen.

"Okay," Scully began. "What the fuck you got going?"

"Well, for one thing, it's a chance for you to make some money and get yourself a decent lawyer. Maybe straighten out this mess you're in. Or at least get yourself some new kicks, you still feel like runnin'. Not that there's anything wrong with those air junkies you got on."

"What is it?" Scully asked.

"Don't worry," Ray said with a smile. "Nothin' to do with swinging a bat or holdin' a hose. Something easy. A little play-acting, you might call it."

Scully squinted at him

"Play, huh?" he asked. "What's my part?"

"Oh, you got a good one. You get to play a cop," Ray said.

"And you?"

"I play myself."

"Two cops, huh? Like a buddy picture," Scully said. "Who else?"

"A rich guy in the city, a CEO. He gets to play himself, too."

"You're askin' what's goin' on with *me?*" Scully said.

"Relax, Scullboy. All we're gonna do is persuade a guy to pay for something that might be real damaging to him."

"Blackmail," Scully said.

"Persuasion, Scull. Persuasion. Just gotta show the guy we mean business. Strappin' guy like yourself could come in handy. After we clean you up a bit, get you a bowl of soup maybe."

Scully chugged his beer and wiped his mouth. He pulled up the sleeves of his cheap sweater. There was a handcuff on each wrist.

"Well," he said. "It ain't like I'm in any position to argue here."

"How the fuck did you get them cut?" Ray asked.

"After I ran off the bus, I hopped a turnstile and got on a train down to Chelsea. I convinced a guy in a hardware store I was a fag who'd gotten mugged. He sawed them off for me. I hopped the turnstile back here right after. I slept in the park last night and came into the Sportsmen this morning for a helping hand."

Ray clicked his beer can against Scully's and smiled.

"Well, you found it, partner. What's that song in the kid movie? 'You've Got a Friend in Me'? Well, you got a friend in ol' Ray here, motherfucker. I'm gonna make you rich."

Scully glanced out the window. It overlooked a lot where a bunch of kids were chasing a dog. One of them picked up a bottle and hurled it as the dog shot into the brush.

Partner, Scully thought. Maybe there is no bottom.

CHAPTER SIXTEEN

BRENT FINISHED TYING his bow tie, looked at himself in the mirror, and smiled. The tuxedo, an Armani, had run him twenty-three hundred dollars, more than the cost of the pickup truck he'd driven to his high school prom, the first time he'd ever worn one.

Martine appeared in the mirror's reflection behind him.

The dress she wore was tight and black and low cut. She wore her hair up and had on a choker of pearls. He buried his face in the nape of her graceful, fragrant neck. He could feel her hip bones through the thin silky fabric, the line of her thong.

His prom date, Susie Arbuckle, wore braces and tasted like cheese when he kissed her, if he remembered right.

The phone rang. He lifted the receiver.

"Yes?"

"Limo's here, Mr. Brent."

It was the doorman.

"We'll be right down," he said.

They got into the elevator and went down to the lobby. On their way to the limo, they passed an architect who was on the building's board. He was in his fifties and wearing a dapper gray suit. He took in Martine as if his eyeballs might roll out of his head.

What was the man's name? Brent thought. Something pompous. William something the third. Brent couldn't resist.

"Night, Bill," he said casually.

Once inside the car, Brent poured himself a scotch as Martine played with the radio and the TV. She opened the sunroof at one point and stood up through it. He smiled and shook his head. Why not? he thought. Limos were supposed to be fun. But when he heard some masculine howls from a street corner, he pulled her back in. As they came to Fifth, Brent saw flashing lights and slowing traffic ahead.

"What is it?" Brent asked the driver.

"Some type of accident," he said.

As they pulled closer, Brent realized that the lights were roaming klieg lights stationed outside the museum, their destination.

"What is this? The Academy Awards?" the driver asked.

Flashbulbs went off in bursts as they stepped onto the sidewalk. Brent showed the silver-embossed invite to a thick-necked security man, who led them past a velvet rope. There was a red carpet draping the massive steps of the museum. Some type of outside light system had been set up, and laser images shimmered upon the pale granite. The huge stonework masks above the entranceway flickered red and yellow and green. At the top, he stopped and took in the rarefied commotion, the lights of the traffic creeping by on Fifth. A week ago, he would have thought this ridiculous. But now, he could appreciate it. He squeezed Martine's hand.

"Well?" he said.

Martine frowned.

"So far okay, I guess," she said.

Inside the doorway, another security guard stood at a podium. Brent gave him his name. He checked a list and handed Brent his seating card with a smile. In the luxuriant shadows, you could make out tuxedos, sequins, champagne glasses, the soft, burning sparkle of gems. The music of violins drifted toward them.

Brent closed his eyes for a moment.

It was like a dream, wasn't it? he thought. To be here now. After almost losing it all, he could see it now, the arc of his life, like some Hollywood plot. Rags to riches. Pauper to prince.

He grabbed a couple of glasses of champagne off the silver tray of a passing waiter and handed one to Martine. He winked at her.

"Life," he said.

They clinked glasses and drank.

Brent looked at the faces in the crowd. A few he recognized from financial magazines.

They wandered into one of the galleries. Headless trunks of Greek statues were lit dramatically on pedestals.

The music stopped suddenly, and a female voice announced, "May I have your attention, please? If everyone would take their seats in the West Room."

They wandered out of the gallery and followed the crowd down a wide corridor that led to an immense, high-ceilinged stone chamber. Fifty circular, linen-covered tables had been arranged before a raised dais with a podium. A gargantuan, colorful abstract painting was lit along the back wall. Brent found their table and they sat. A few minutes later, the lights dimmed, and the crowd became quiet. A woman went up to the podium and introduced all the members on the function's board. Brent took it all in, the colorful mural burning in the darkness behind him, the rich, sweet aroma of perfume, the pale fire of Martine's throat. You were supposed to hate these functions. But he didn't.

"Tonight," said the skeletal female emcee from the podium in a high, refined voice, "we have a special treat. Dancers from the Broadway smash *Leather* are here to per-form for us tonight at this special function. Without further ado, I give you *Leather.*"

A spotlight went on in the darkness before the painting. A white man in a skintight black bodysuit stepped into it and did a pirouette as some type of African music started. Soon another man, this one black in a skintight white bodysuit, joined him. They danced around each other. The black man lifted the white one up.

"Preventin' AIDS?" said a southern voice at Brent's elbow. "Looks more like they're spreadin' it to me."

It was the man seated to the left of him.

Nobody laughed. Brent kept watching the performance as if he hadn't heard a thing.

After the dancers, waiters appeared and took their dinner orders. People from the dais stood at intervals and spoke at the podium about the charity, something to do with AIDS and children. Brent hardly paid attention. When a speaker called his name, he didn't even notice. Martine nudged him in the ribs.

"Brent. Mr. Robert Brent," he heard.

For a disorienting split second, he believed that he'd won something. Businessman of the Year, perhaps.

When he heard, "Phone call. Emergency phone call for Mr. Robert Brent at the front desk," his stomach hit the ground.

Guest, he thought immediately. Something had gone wrong.

Martine looked at him, perplexed.

"I'll be right back," he told her.

He could feel the doubtful eyes of the crowd shift his way in the darkness as he stood. Emergency phone call: faux pas, he heard them thinking. He entered the corridor. At the desk, the security guard and two other men stared at him as he approached. One was short and squat with a shaved head and a mean face. The other was black-haired and tall. Both wore cheap, ill-fitting suits. Brent looked at the security guard, who looked away.

"You Robert Brent?" said the short one.

"Yes."

The tall one grabbed Brent's hands.

"Hey, what the . . ." Brent said, recoiling instinctively.

A badge appeared before his eyes as a handcuff clicked down around his wrist.

"You're under arrest," the squat one announced. "You have the right to remain silent. . . ."

"Get your . . ." Brent wriggled out of the tall one's grip. The short one hit him with something small and incredibly hard behind his ear. Brent froze in pain.

"Hey, you want to do this the hard way?" the short one rasped at him. "We could do this the hard way."

Brent relaxed. The tall one bent his arm behind him and clicked on the other cuff.

"As I was saying," the short one continued, "you have the right to remain silent."

"What! Why? This is ridiculous. For what?"

"Hey, I just collect you scumbags. I don't ask what for."

"I want my lawyer!" Brent screamed.

"Hey, listen up," the short one said, grabbing him by his lapels. "You wanna make a scene, I'll drag you down those front steps in fucking leg shackles. You wanna see yourself on the cover of the *Daily News?* You'll get a phone call at the station. If you didn't do nothin' wrong, you got nothin' to worry about."

"Hey, wait, wait! My girlfriend is in there. I have to let her know," Brent said.

"Hey, I did you a favor by callin' you out here. You want to go back into the party again, it's gonna be with those cuffs on."

Brent turned to the security man as the two cops led him off.

"Tell my girlfriend, please. The tall, French girl. Where are you taking me? Where are we going?" he asked the short cop.

They came to a stairwell door. The short cop banged him through it.

"Enough outta you," he said. "Now, where the fuck was I?"

"He's got the right to remain silent," the tall one said.

"That's right," said the short one, taking him out an exit door. An unmarked, blue Chevy stood at the little service road at the back of the museum. They rushed him toward it. Unbelievable. Oh, my God, unbelievable, Brent thought.

"Anything you say not only can, but actually *will,* be used against you in a court of law," the cop explained.

RAY LOOKED INTO the rearview mirror at Brent. The CEO leaned against the door, pale and stunned. No more complaints out of you, huh? Ray thought. Guilt and fear were eating at him now. They had him, Ray knew. The clammy stench of bitch coming off him was overpowering.

Ray glanced at Scully looking blankly out the window beside him as they drove north in the park. Boy was holding up better than he'd expected. Telling him where he'd lost his place was good, solid straight-man shit. No doubt about it, their fish was hooked.

He drove the rental car up to the Seventy-second Street Drive and made a left, heading west through Central Park.

Earlier in the day, Ray had called up one of his old partners from the day shift and gotten him to bring up Brent's address off the cruiser's DMV computer. They'd gone to Brent's apartment first, hoping to catch him sitting down to dinner, the element of shock being essential. When the doorman ratted that he and his girl had gone to this party, Ray figured, so much the better. Getting the super-buff security guard to have him called out for a phone call had been a piece of cake. If they'd dragged Brent naked out of the shower, Ray doubted that they could've shaken him up more. He glanced back at Brent again, concealing a smile. Goddamn, he was starting to enjoy this.

They went over to Columbus and made a left heading south. It became Ninth Avenue after Fifty-ninth Street and they drove into Hell's Kitchen. They approached the back of Port Authority, passing a shadowed assemblage of derelicts on the sidewalk, made another left down a darkened block in the Garment District and slowed before the ugly brick box of the Midtown South Precinct. Ray pulled into a parking space near the front and cut the engine. A uniformed sergeant on his way in the front door gave them a wave. Ray returned the gesture as Scully stiffened beside him. Ray opened his door.

He wasn't about to take Brent in there, but Brent didn't know that. The point was to make him think they were going in. Rile him up.

"Hey, you know what?" Ray said to Scully. "I feel like a doughnut or something. You want a doughnut?"

"Now that you mention it," Scully said, recovering. "I could go for a cruller."

"Yeah," Ray said, closing the door. "Let those Feds wait five minutes, right?" he said, making it up as he went along. "I mean, it's not like we're gonna get any credit for this collar anyway. We bring him in too early, they'll just send us out to collect another one."

Ray started the car up again and backed out.

"It's not like Mr. Rich Guy here gives a fuck. Right, Mr. Brent? It's Robert, right? Ah, what the hell. Let me call ya Robbie. You're gonna have to get used to not standin' on too much ceremony from here on in anyway. There's an all-night bakery around the corner, Robbie. It ain't your Starbucks, maybe, but at least you don't have to take out a mortgage to get a cup of joe."

They pulled around the corner, stopped at a brightly lit sidewalk counter, and Scully got out. When he returned with a white sack, they headed west through the thinning traffic and drove south again into the twenties. They turned right between darkened, steel-shuttered warehouses onto an empty, rough cobblestone street and stopped. A dark form sat up on an elevated loading dock, yawned, and lay back down.

"I think you woke him up," Scully commented, taking a sip of his coffee.

"Yeah?" Ray said. "Man's gotta expect a little disturbance if he likes to use the curb for a pillow. Isn't that right, Rob? You look like a good Republican."

"I want my lawyer," Brent said angrily.

"Uh-oh. I think he's pissed," Scully said.

"Some people are so ungrateful," Ray said. "Here we are postponing this asshole's trip to the slammer and he's complaining. Fine, Robbie," Ray said, putting down his coffee. "You want to go to jail? Let's go to jail."

"I just want to get this cleared up."

"I'm sure you do, Robbie," Ray said with a laugh. He looked at Brent in the rearview. "I'm sure you fucking do. Good luck, though. I mean with all those dead El Salvadorans and all."

Ray watched Brent's eyes bug out. "Bribing government officials to cover it up. I hope you can get out of this, Robbie. I really do. You're gonna need a good lawyer, though. I mean, a really good lawyer."

"Johnnie Cochran," Scully offered.

"El Salvadorans?" Brent said, his voice threatening to crack. "What are you talking about?"

Ray turned around in his seat and smiled slowly at Brent. He nodded toward Scully, who produced a tape recorder and hit *play.*

"Mr. Guest. What can I do for you?" Brent's amplified

voice asked. They sat there and listened to the rest of the conversation. When it was over, Ray held up a finger and hit *rewind*. After a few seconds, he hit *play* again.

"Do what you have to do," Brent's voice said again. "Make this go away."

Ray hit *stop*. He smirked, shaking his head.

"That's my favorite part. That's some callous shit. The fucking Dream Team isn't gonna make that sound good."

"Who? What is this?" Brent asked.

"Okay, Robbie. No more fuckin' around," Ray said, looking him in the eye. "We know what happened down in El Salvador. We also know about your merger and how you don't want to get that all fucked up. Now *you* know we know it. Question is, what do you want to do about it? You sounded pretty eager to pay off those bean eaters running the show down in the jungle to get this smelling right. We just want in on the action. You think I want to see you go to the slammer with the newspapers screaming about how your company's responsible for offing all those little brown muchachos? Because I don't. Every Paco who can swing a shank or get a hard-on is gonna want a piece of your ass, and let me tell you, there's a lot of them in your incarcerated population. I should know. I put quite a few of them there myself. I don't want to do that. I want to cut a deal with you, and I'm gonna make it easy. You pay, you walk. That simple. Seven hundred thousand in unmarked hundreds in three days or I turn the tape over to the federal attorney general for the Southern District, but not before it goes over to the *New York Times*, *Daily News*, and *New York Post*. You heard me. *New York Post*, okay? Think about Page Six with your face in the cartoon."

Ray held the tape recorder in his palm. Scully took his cue

to get out and open up the rear door. He unlocked Brent's cuffs, and then got back in the front seat.

"You see this, Robbie?" Ray said, hefting the recorder. "This here's your nuts. Seven hundred thousand gets them back. We'll call you. Now get the fuck out of my car."

Brent stepped out.

"Three days," Ray told him, and he hit the gas and they were out of there.

"Did you see the fucking look on his face when I said 'dead El Salvadorans'?" Ray asked Scully with a grin as they tooled north on the West Side Highway, heading home. "I thought he was gonna shit himself."

Let's see, Scully thought. Kidnapping, impersonating an officer, blackmail. Pretty soon he'd be holding up liquor stores. One thing was certain. Ray was crazy. The guy had never been too stable as a kid, but now look at him. He was actually enjoying himself.

"I'd say we got his attention," Scully agreed.

Jesus Christ, Scully thought. He had actually cuffed the poor sap. Made good on his side of the Mutt-and-Jeff routine to terrorize the son of a bitch. And what was really surprising was learning that Ray's brother, Sean, was the one who had come up with the tape in the first place. The guy had a sick wife and he was involving himself in this crazy shit? The whole fucking world had gone mad.

Got to ride this out, Scully told himself, looking out at the lights of the GW Bridge looming on their left. Look for the right place to jump off and then just go. This was heavier than anything he wanted to be involved in.

"You did great, my man." Ray smiled as they drove along. "You would have made a decent cop."

"Hey, don't insult me," Scully said.

"That fucker's gonna cough," Ray said earnestly in the dark. "I can feel it."

Scully took out a cigarette and lit it.

"What makes you so sure he won't go to the FBI?"

"It would be retarded of him, and let me tell you, this guy didn't get to where he is by being retarded."

"Seven hundred K is pretty large money to come up with in three days, though. Don't you think?"

"You heard that tape," Ray said. "Guy's got some type of slush account down in Mexico. He'll just have to make another withdrawal. Hey, don't be fucking doubting this shit now. The fun's about to begin."

"I'm not doubting you," Scully said, dragging from his cigarette. "I'm just playing devil's advocate."

"You just leave all that devil shit to me, all right?" Ray said.

Scully was silent.

"You got it," he said.

Just like I thought, Scully mused as they pulled off their exit. This guy's a fuckin' loon.

CHAPTER SEVENTEEN

SEAN MACKLIN TOOK a sip of his coffee as he rolled his phone truck up darkened Tenth Avenue. Puckett napped against the passenger-side door. They'd just been dispatched on a cable failure on the East Side, and they were making their way there as fast as the outdated vehicle would allow.

He felt good, having spoken to his brother that morning. He'd never felt terrific about his nocturnal activities, but now that it seemed something good might come out them, he felt calm for the first time in a long while. For one night, it seemed he could just concentrate on the job he was paid for and was good at: fixing lines.

He made a right on Forty-sixth and drove crosstown. Five minutes later, he pulled up in front of an almost windowless building between Second and First. In the stone above its steel door, a small bell with a circle around it was carved along with the words: EMPIRE TEL.

Puckett awakened as Macklin shut off the engine. From the back of the truck, Macklin retrieved two items, a small bag about the size of a camera and a heavy plastic square box. They crossed the street to the central office. Macklin took out his electronic access card and laid it upon the glass box recessed in the wall next to the steel entrance door, and it clicked open.

They took the elevator up to the fourth floor. They stepped into a wide corridor with stainless steel wainscoting and rubber bumpers to accommodate large equipment. Metal doors marked with cryptic numbers and letters fell away to each side. Macklin stopped before one, punched the combination on the lock, and opened the door.

They stepped onto the main frame. The lights were connected to a motion detector, and they tripped on like dominoes through the long room as they walked in.

Wall to wall, it had to be a hundred and fifty feet long. A massive, freestanding, modern sculpture of exposed wire and naked steel. Set from the floor to ceiling, down the length of the immense room, were vertical binding posts that held numbered pins. Wired into these pins was every phone line from Forty-fourth to Sixty-second Streets, from Fifth Avenue to the East River.

"Okay," Macklin said. "This is called the frame. It's where the lines for the whole district converge and are sorted."

"*Every* line in the district area is in this room?" Puckett said.

"Every one. This is the first place you come when they give you a trouble ticket. Now . . ."

"Wait," Puckett said. "You mean, if I lived in the area and

you had my phone number, you could just come into this room and access my line?"

"Um-hmm," Macklin said.

"Has anybody ever gotten in trouble for listening in on someone?" Puckett said.

Macklin bristled for a moment.

"Sure. Don't you read the security bulletins? Guys get busted for listening in on their girlfriends or bringing up their LUDs.

"What's an LUD?"

"Local usage details, the list of every call that was made from your phone in a given period. Only long distance calls are posted on your bill. LUDs are secret, and only the cops have access to them during a criminal investigation. You know the paper Matlock pulls out on TV and says, 'On the night of your wife's murder, why did you make three calls to your secretary's house?' That's the LUDs. You can pull them up in the control center if you know what you're doing. A phone guy's wife gotta be real discreet."

"Wow," Puckett said. "I never thought about that."

"Sure," Macklin said. "There's plenty of trouble you can get into. There was a switchman one time who was listening to the radio, right? And there's a contest: ninety-first caller wins front-row tickets. He knew the radio station was in district, so he brings the number up on his computer and counts the calls coming in. After the ninetieth one, he opens the line at the switch so no other calls can come in and dials up. 'What? I won?' he says. 'Get outta here. I never won anything in my life.'"

"No! He get caught?"

"Coworker ratted him out."

Puckett shook his head and looked at the frame.

"I never knew we were so powerful," he said.

Macklin was silent for a long moment.

"We got work to do," he said, holding up the paper.

"You see here on the ticket where they give you the cable and pair? Well, what you do is look up by the ceiling until you find your cable, and then go down the binding posts until you get your pair."

Macklin began walking down one of the corridors with Puckett. He stopped before a row of binding posts.

"You see? It says two-two-six-six cable up there. That's the one we want. Look here," Macklin pointed to some numbers. "You see how the individual lines are marked? We look for the pair on the ticket."

Macklin pointed to a pair of pins.

"Here it is. Next, take the KS meter."

Macklin opened the camera-sized bag and took out a set of leads and clipped them to the pins.

"Clip this sucker to your pair. Now, a little background. You know those things in the manholes that look like snakes?"

"The cables?" Puckett said with a laugh.

"Right, the cables. Well, inside of them are thin copper wires that go from here all the way to the customer. Do you know how a telephone works?"

"Yeah," Puckett said uneasily.

"Really? I've been working here six years and it's still fucking magic to me. But you know what? I don't have to know. Because all I care about are the cables and the lines inside them, keeping them connected and keeping them dry. Phone lines might as well be made of fucking string, as far as you and I are concerned. Our job is to keep the strings connected and dry. You understand?"

"So far so good."

"Great. Right now, we're looking at the line in the street." Macklin clicked a switch on the meter and pointed at the gauge. "You see it stick? That means it's wet. What we want to do is find three or four other lines that look the same."

Macklin quickly clipped and reclipped the leads onto several other lines. He found three more pairs.

"Okay. We have three bad pairs that all kind of look the same. Now comes the fun part."

Macklin opened the plastic box and clipped its brightly colored leads across the bad line.

"This is a breakdown set and it'll zap six hundred thirty volts across the wires, welding them together where it's wet. Once they're welded, we can get a distance reading and put a tone on the line that we can hear with a special microphone. Then we get to go out and start popping covers, chasing the tone along the cable until it stops. Where it stops is where it's wet."

"What do you do when you find it?" Puckett said.

"You open up the cable, resplice the line you broke in and then dry out the rest of the cable."

"Once it's dry, the magic is happy again?" Puckett said.

Macklin punched his partner in the shoulder.

"You're gonna make foreman in no time," he said.

Macklin zapped the pairs and got distance readings.

"Three thousand feet," Macklin said, switching on the tone. "Let's go out and check the address on the ticket."

THE ADDRESS WAS a silver door off Madison with a velvet rope in front of it. Two well-dressed men emerged with a blast of techno music as Macklin parked in front.

Macklin went to the back of the truck and took down what looked like a computer mouse hooked into a unit with earphones. He walked over to the club's entrance and knocked on the door. The man who opened it was black and shirtless and extremely muscular. He wore eye shadow and nipple rings.

"Yeah?" he said.

Macklin blinked and showed his ID.

"Ah, phone company, pal. How you doin'? I was wondering if we might be able to get access to your basement. We're tryin' to find some trouble you got on your cable."

The bouncer looked out at the truck.

"Hold on."

He spoke into a walkie-talkie.

"Boss said sure, if you want to wait ten minutes," the bouncer said.

"No problem," Macklin said.

They stood inside by a stairwell. The music that pounded up sounded like a pile driver slamming down steel beams for the foundation of a building.

Macklin nudged Puckett with his elbow. He gestured with his chin toward the bouncer.

"C'mon, stop pretending. Introduce me to your friend," he said.

"Bite me," Puckett said.

After a while, a thin, effeminate man came up and escorted them downstairs. The club was hot and pitch black except for the firefight of lights that intermittently exploded back and forth across the length of the low-ceilinged chamber. Sweating, shirtless men writhed on the packed dance floor. Macklin turned around and shook his head at Puckett.

"Run," he said.

Back up top, they thanked the bouncer.

"No way we were gonna hear tone in that shit," Macklin said. "We're gonna have to pop the first hole in the street and start looking there."

The hole was up the block toward Fifth. Puckett backed the truck up, and they popped the hole, put in the rail, and dropped down a light and the blower. It was a nasty-smelling sidewalk hole. Thick, dark slime covered the cables and was caked around the rim.

He certainly wasn't in any rush to go down there. He remembered Brent's tap and had an idea.

"Listen, you wait here while the hole purges. I'm gonna walk back to the central office and make sure the six-thirty is still on. I'm not going down into that shit to look for tone, only to find some jerkoff frameman back at the CO switched it off."

"They'd do that?"

"Those sons of bitches will do anything," Macklin said, ducking out under the tape. "I'll be right back."

He walked down an empty Forty-fourth to Vanderbilt and then made a right along Grand Central Station. He crossed over Forty-second and walked down to Park. He looked around and, seeing no one, crossed the street toward the recession in the slope of the viaduct. He took out his key and opened the door. In the darkness on the floor off to his left was the bag that he'd left there with his flashlight and tools.

He found the bag with his foot and took out the flashlight and turned it on. He walked quietly through the threshold and keyed open the lock on the vault door. He walked quickly in the murky dark beneath and between the cables until he

reached the north end of one of the corridors where they disappeared into the wall.

At intervals along the cables were splice cases: fat, plastic
cylinders where you could access the wires inside. The splice
case where he'd placed Brent's tap was marked with orange
safety tape. He found it quickly, lifted a metal cable hanger off
the floor, and knocked off the locking bars. Then he popped
off the plastic shell.

He stood looking at the wires. It didn't look like anything
really, he thought, gazing at the tangled splice, like a rat's nest
of colored string. But one pair of wires had been culled from
the bunch. Attached to them was what looked like a fat orange
marker stuck to a small tape recorder. Laid against the bare
wires as it was, the tap picked up anything said over the line,
and the voice-activated cassette player recorded it. It was a
crude, but effective, bug. The best thing about it was that it
worked on the electrical field that surrounded the wires, without coming into actual physical contact with them. So even if
the line was swept for bugs, as he had read many executives'
lines were, it couldn't be detected.

Without disturbing the wires, Macklin removed the bug
from the line and put it into his pocket carefully. Then he
quickly replaced the case.

He heard a thump as he headed out. He panicked for a
second, unable to determine if it had come from outside. He
slid off his bag and stuffed it beneath some cables. He inched
his way forward through the dark to the door and peeked
out. There was nobody there. It'd probably just been a passing car above. He considered going back for the bag, but
changed his mind. He locked the vault door and stepped for
the exit.

It took him less than twenty minutes to get back to the manhole.

Puckett looked up from the back bumper where he sat.

"Everything okay, now?" he said.

Macklin smiled.

"Peachy keen," he said.

CHAPTER EIGHTEEN

FROM A BALCONY above Times Square, Guest swirled his wine and looked down at the lights.

There was something heartening in the billion-watt glow, he thought, something earnest in the bright, pulsing geysers. It'd been what since he'd seen them last? Fifteen? No, eighteen years. It'd been the summer of '82, right before they shipped him out to Afghanistan. He could remember graffiti, hookers, garbage on the sidewalks, aggressive packs of inner-city youths swarming out of arcades and sex shops. It was much cleaner now, he'd noticed happily, the streets better lit, less dangerous. Whoever was responsible should be commended. Creating order out of chaos wasn't an easy job.

He knew that firsthand.

He'd arrived two hours earlier on a flight that had stopped

over in Miami. It was an eight-hour trip, and he'd been happy to arrive finally in New York. He was even more pleased at the disinterest the customs agent at Kennedy gave his forged passport as he stamped it. He'd gotten it from a contractor in Mexico City that he'd never used before. It was nice to discover someone who did good work.

He used the fake passport, not because he wasn't a citizen, but because he was wanted by federal officials on some matters. This was a business trip. He didn't need the distraction, and as a businessman now, the client always came first.

He looked past the open door into his room. The heavy furniture, the thick carpet, the hunter green curtains. He was on the concierge floor, and there was a bar, a coffee machine, stationery, and the day's paper on the desk. There was a strip of cardboard around the toilet seat in the bathroom. There was even a hotel movie channel on the TV where you could order porno movies whose titles wouldn't appear on your credit card bill. It had everything he admired about corporate America: comfort, cleanliness, efficiency. He'd read all the arguments on the vapidity of the new American marketing culture, how it bled out meaning and blah-blah-blah, but he didn't buy it. Living in jungles and war zones turned one on pretty quickly to the simple joys of convenience, to comfort that was free of germs and vacuum-packed.

He glanced at a folder on the desk that contained his typed report along with the appropriate receipts. He smiled as he checked his watch. Nine P.M. He lifted his wine and finished it. He debated whether to have another.

No, he decided, putting the glass down, he'd hold off.

Everything in moderation.

He turned to the window and smiled at the dancing lights.

* * *

THE TIMES SQUARE Palms's lobby was crowded. A giddy group of high school girls from Ohio, by their letter jackets, was checking in, so Brent had to wait. They kept looking back at him in his tuxedo and giggling, excited about their class trip to the big city, no doubt. He just returned an icy glare and waited for them to clear out.

He'd been *blindsided!* What the hell did the cops want with him? And, why the hell was there a tap on his phone? Was he under some type of investigation?

When he'd gotten back to the museum in a taxi, he'd found Martine near tears on the sidewalk.

"The man said you were arrested," she'd cried, running over to him.

"It was a huge mistake," he'd told her. "Someone's playing games with me."

"To have you arrested?"

"I have some really funny friends," he'd said, and left it at that. She could believe him or not. He didn't have time to care. He'd dropped her off back at the apartment and come straight to Times Square.

When the pubescent rubes were finally gone, Brent stepped up to the young male desk clerk and barked, "Mr. Guest. What room?"

The clerk looked up, startled. The bracing slap of New York demand after so much Midwestern nicety seemed to have knocked him off balance. Brent could see him mustering a protest, but then reconsidering when faced with Brent's steely gaze.

He tapped some keys on the computer before him.

"Six-oh-eight," he said, without looking up.

Brent took the elevator to the sixth floor and stepped into the carpeted hall.

Could things possibly get worse? he thought. It was inconceivable. Someone actually had a tape of him. A clear, irrefutable record of him covering up the El Salvadoran thing.

Could he actually be arrested? Under what charges? That didn't really matter anyway, did it? They might as well toss him in a cell, the way the bottom would drop out of his life if the tape came out.

He reached 608 and knocked.

The man who opened the door was medium-sized and slim. The dark suit he wore was plain, but well-cut. His silver hair was combed straight back on his skull and his clean-shaven, pale face was neither attractive nor unattractive, without distinction but for the eyes, which were gunmetal gray and possessed of an exceptional gravity. Eyes that missed nothing and showed less.

"Mr. Brent," Guest said. His voice was as flat as on the telephone. He extended his hand. Brent shook it. Guest's hand was surprisingly large and rough. The grip of a carpenter, he thought, a stonemason.

"I wasn't expecting you until later," Guest said, stepping aside. There was a formality in his manner that made Brent momentarily forget his agitation and remember his manners.

"I'm sorry. Did I come at a bad time?" Brent asked as he walked in. He saw a room service cart set up by the window. A tray with a wine bottle and plate sat on top of it.

"Don't be silly," Guest said, quietly walking over to the cart. "Please sit."

Brent sat on a chair by the dresser. Guest lifted the bottle.

"Can I pour you a glass of wine?"

"No, thank you," Brent said, spying a wet bar over by the bed. "Drop of scotch would be great, though."

Guest went to the bar, flipped up a highball glass, and caught it adroitly with his long fingers. He poured a small amber measure and handed Brent the glass.

"As I told you earlier, we were quite successful with the El Salvadoran authorities."

Guest went to his night table and came back with a plastic-covered report.

Brent went over it quickly, nodding. Then he closed the folder and knocked back the scotch. He stared at the empty glass in his hand.

"Very good," Brent said. "Except we have another problem now. A big one."

Guest was raising his wineglass to his lips.

"Oh?"

"I was arrested an hour ago by two police officers. They played me a tape of our conversation from two days ago and offered to sell it back to me."

Guest's expression changed. He leaned forward slightly. Brent had gotten his attention.

"Or what?"

"They'd turn it over to the Feds and bring it to the papers," Brent explained.

"Hmm," Guest said, putting down his wineglass and looking off toward the window. He said nothing for a full minute. Then he got up, turned on the television full volume. He closed the curtains before he sat back down. The loud sound of canned laughter filled the room. Guest moved his chair over and leaned forward until their knees were almost touching.

"Were they real policemen?" Guest said.

"Yes. No. I don't know. They weren't in uniform, but they had badges and handcuffs. The car they put me in was a Chevy, like an unmarked police car. We parked in front of a precinct and they waved at some cops going in. If they were actors, they were good."

"Hmmm," Guest said again. "How much did they want?"

"Seven hundred thousand. Who the hell is doing this to me?" Brent asked.

"I don't know. But we'll find out. Did you see any names or badge numbers?"

"No. Do you think I should pay them?" Brent asked.

"First, we have to determine what they're capable of doing. I made the recommendation for investment in El Salvador because we can trust the people we're dealing with to uphold their end of the bargain. The men who just did this to you are a mystery to us. Their methods are crude, so that's some advantage. I suggest that we find out who were dealing with."

"How are we going to do that?"

"There are ways. How long did they give you to find the money?"

"Three days."

"All right," Guest said. "That doesn't give us much time."

"You can find them?" Brent asked.

"If they're real police officers, yes."

"How?"

"Police academy yearbooks," Guest said quickly. "How old were they?"

Brent nodded. He hadn't thought of that. He liked the man's directness.

"I don't know. Early thirties."

"Okay. We'll assume they were at least twenty when they

joined, so we'll go back fifteen years and start there. We'll also concentrate on men who are now in the NYPD electronics division, police who would have access to phone-tapping equipment. I'll get pictures and you can pick them out. Call me back from an outside pay phone after I contact you, all right? Better yet, I'll pick up a set of cell phones with scramblers."

"Okay," Brent said.

"If it comes down to it, can the payment be arranged?" asked Guest.

"I can take care of that end," Brent said. The Mexican account wasn't the only slush fund they had.

Guest refilled Brent's glass.

Brent began to feel better, less uncertain. Offense was always the best defense.

"If we do this, you understand no authorities will be informed. We'll be acting on our own accord. If you have a problem with that, you must tell me now," Guest said.

Brent looked at him gravely. What had Mitch told him? Guest was the only one not burned by Iran-Contra. Brent pictured the cop again. The way he'd put his hands on him. The cocksureness of his ultimatum.

Brent's knuckles were white against the highball glass. He knocked the scotch back.

"That's your field of expertise, Mr. Guest. I'll leave you to it," he said.

Guest considered his employer's answer and nodded in satisfaction.

"Consider it done," Guest said. His eyes flickered with the light from the TV.

CHAPTER NINETEEN

IT WAS RAINING the morning of the pickup, a cold, steady downpour that kept the world dark. Ray listened to it drumroll on the roof of the rented Chevy while he waited for Scully to come out of the bodega. In the store window, there was a cardboard cutout of Frankenstein carrying a case of Bud, the Spanish word *chotacabras* written in marker above it. As bad as his Spanish was, Ray recognized the word. It meant "goat-sucker," a type of vampire monster that sucked animals' blood and ate babies, a Latin American Bigfoot. Ray looked down the block where a hooded fifteen-year-old heroin dealer huddled in a rancid tenement doorway. As if they had to invent human bloodsuckers around here, he thought.

Scully emerged a moment later from the store with a brown sack.

"There better not be any hooch in there," Ray said as Scully got in.

Scully took a cardboard coffee cup from the bag for Ray and one for himself. He took out a pack of cigarettes and got one lit.

"Hooch?" he said. "You're lucky I don't make you pick me up some angel dust with what we're about to do."

"What are you talkin' about?" Ray said. "Everything's set. Plus, with the getaway plan you concocted, things can't go wrong. Stop being such a pussy."

Scully guffawed into his coffee. "Okay. We'll see how tough you are when C-block's pullin' a train on you in the fucking big house."

"Hey," Ray said, putting the car into drive and pulling out, "even if we do get caught, I'm not worried. I'll just wait for you to figure a way to bust us out."

Scully squinted at the rain, dragged on his cigarette, and flicked ashes out the crack in the window.

Ray had called Brent the night before from a pay phone and given him the instructions. They would do the exchange at a quarter after noon on the sidewalk across from Brent's office building on Park. It was a little after ten o'clock now, but they wanted to get downtown a little early. They had a couple of things to set up first.

Brent seemed more amiable on the phone, more willing to make a deal. Ray imagined it wasn't the first time he'd used his checkbook as an eraser.

They drove west toward the city in silence. Tenements and projects passed by in intervals out of the gray haze. Ray thought about his brother. He still felt like a prick for using the tape. But come on, he thought. Sean's line of thinking was childish. Make the bad rich guy pay for his crime. Yeah, he'd pay for it all right. Pay his lawyers and the judge maybe. To imagine that the death of a bunch of El Salvadorans meant a damn thing to anybody was wishful thinking in this cold, cruel world.

They entered Manhattan over the rusted Willis Avenue Bridge. They took Fifth through Harlem's empty streets, passing by dark forms grouped in the doorways of tattered, stately buildings. Past Ninety-sixth, he made a left and headed over to Lex. Yellow cabs and brake lights were jammed to the cramped horizon.

It was nearly eleven when they turned onto Forty-fifth Street. They drove up the block until they were almost directly beneath the elevated roadway of the Park Avenue Viaduct. They pulled over to the side of the street and double-parked. Ray had gotten a spinning red dashboard light from a cop store, and he plugged it into the cigarette lighter and they got out.

The Park Avenue Viaduct was the elevated roadway that ran north-south around Grand Central Station and the MetLife Building, connecting Park Avenue South to Park Avenue. Passing trucks growled loudly under the green-painted iron bridge as he and Scully searched the surface of the street.

"There," Scully said, pointing to a grate on the sidewalk just outside the overpass.

Ray came over, bent, and peered into the darkness through its bars.

"You're sure?" he asked him.

"Positive," Scully said.

Ray looked at the grate and then took a step back and looked up at the elevated roadway above, gauging the distance, the angle.

He smiled.

"All right," he told Scully.

They walked back to the car and popped the trunk. They took out two crowbars and some orange traffic cones that Ray had commandeered from a roadway worksite. There was a large backpack in there as well, and Scully strapped it on. They stepped back over to the grate and placed the cones around it. Then they slid the curved part of the crowbars in through the grate and pulled. The grate swung up and back with a clang. Though it was raining, there were a lot of people passing on that busy block. Not one of them paid any attention.

Ray leaned into the dark space. He could just make out tracks below as the railroad smell of smoke and fuel hit him. He stood back up and handed Scully a cellular phone.

"I'm trustin' you now, Scull," said Ray.

Scully took a step toward the MetLife Building to their left.

"Just make sure you don't miss," Scully called through the rain.

SCULLY MOVED QUICKLY through the MetLife Building. It was almost lunchtime, and an army of people bustled about the stark, white marble lobby. He walked across the mezzanine, past the elevators, and got on the other escalator going down. He stepped off into the main waiting area for Grand Central Station. There were Metro-North train tunnels at the corners, and he stood for a moment in the bustling crowd trying to remember the one he wanted. Then he turned to his left and began to walk.

There were miles of tunnels under the streets around Grand Central, Scully knew. He'd worked in Midtown when he was a rookie in the fire department, and one weekend a year, they'd have emergency drills, mock terrorist attacks to test response times and coordination between all the different departments. One year, their company's task was to rescue people from a trapped train on the track beneath Forty-fifth Street. The grate that he and Ray had just opened was the access they'd used.

He walked down the ramp. There were no trains on either side of the platform, and he walked underground back north toward Forty-fifth. There were some construction workers a few platforms away, but they were busy welding. Scully checked his watch and picked up his pace. He walked for a while and thought that maybe he'd chosen the wrong platform until he heard a splatter in the distance. He approached through the dark, looking up. Thirty feet down, he spotted some grates in the ceiling high above from which rain fell. The one that they'd opened was another couple of feet down, and he stepped beneath it. He could see the traffic cones they'd placed out on the sidewalk and the ornate rail of the Park Avenue Viaduct in the distance above.

He removed the knapsack. He peered into the darkness from where he had come, but couldn't see anyone. If a train pulled in, would the driver notify authorities? He sat on the ground a few feet back out of the rain. He took out his cigarettes, lit one, and cupped it. He exhaled smoke nervously.

"All you now, Ray," he whispered in the dark.

❖   ❖   ❖

A MINUTE LATER Ray brought the sedan to a stop across from Brent's office building. After a while, a brownie directing traffic on the corner of Forty-seventh began to walk over. Ray plugged in his dashboard light again and flashed his badge through the windshield. The traffic cop nodded knowingly, turned on his heel, and walked back.

At ten after, Brent emerged from the building across the street. He wore a raincoat and carried a garment bag, a heavy one it seemed from the strained way he was walking.

Holy shit, Ray thought. It was actually happening! He stifled a smile as he rolled down the window.

"Get in," Ray said as Brent approached.

Brent stopped before the driver's window and looked around.

"No way," he said. "Where's the tape?"

Ray looked over at the sidewalk. He took the small recorder out of his jacket and hit *play*.

"Make this go away," Brent's voice said.

Ray hit *stop*.

"And the money?"

Brent zipped open the bag a couple of inches. Tightly wrapped, bundled cash stared out. Ray's eyes were riveted.

"Chuck it here," Ray said, offering the recorder.

Brent passed over the bag and took the recorder. Ray put the bag on the seat beside him, took out a bundle, and riffled through it quickly. Hundreds all the way through. He looked back at Brent with a wide smile. Brent frowned.

"This is it. You understand that, right?" the CEO said coldly. The recorder was already away in his jacket somewhere. "I'd rather see my face in the paper than to see yours again."

"C'mon, Robbie. Relax," Ray said. "Think of this as just another transaction. At least you're keeping the money within the border, doing your part to keep our economy running strong."

"I better not see you again," Brent said, and walked away quickly.

Ray zipped the bag up tight and looked into his rearview mirror. Some town cars were double-parked behind him. He put the car in drive and gunned out. He plugged in his red light, and the brownie stopped traffic and waved him through Forty-seventh. Ray gave him a thumbs-up as he passed onto the ramp for the viaduct.

He took out his phone and dialed Scully.

"Yeah," Scully answered.

"You ready?" Ray asked him as he exited the tunnel above Forty-fifth Street.

"Yeah."

"Here I come," Ray said, dropping the phone as he slammed on the brakes. He grabbed the money-filled bag, got out, and ran to the rail. Horns from the traffic behind wailed. The open grate was on the street right beneath him, and he draped the heavy bag over the green metal rail and let go. He watched it disappear through the hole.

"Yesss!" he yelled as he jogged back to the car. "You got it?" he shouted into the phone as he put the car into drive again.

"I got it," Scully called back.

"Jordan ain't got nothin' on me, motherfucker," Ray said.

SCULLY SNAPPED THE phone shut and unzipped the black bag that had just dropped like an anvil through the open grate a moment earlier. Tight stacks of hundreds wrapped in orange ribbons lay nestled within. He blinked, dumbfounded. A metallic crash in the tunnel ahead brought him back to reality. He zipped open his own bag, removed a pair of scissors, and began cutting the ribbons and dropping the loose cash into his bag. They wanted to get rid of the bag and ribbons in case some kind of transmitter had been inserted that could be used to track them down. There were seventy bundles in all, and by the time he was done three minutes later, sweat was pouring off him.

He zipped up the knapsack, swung it onto his back, and stood. The weight of it was incredible. He left the garment bag where it lay and kicked the ribbons onto the tracks. He walked quickly down the platform, keeping his eyes to the lit threshold that led back into Grand Central ahead.

Everything seemed extraordinarily normal when he walked back into the waiting area. A few feet away, a Chinese girl played a violin. It took a minute of her beautiful piece to convince him that she wasn't an undercover FBI agent. He began to walk across the plaza and blend with the crowd. He looked up at the massive dome of the refurbished ceiling, at the white star constellations swirling in a cosmos of rich money green.

He was getting away with it!

He spotted the sign for the Bronx subway in the corner of the room by a doorway. As he made his way toward it, the strains of violin behind him began to soar.

RAY GLANCED INTO his rearview mirror right before he turned into the underground garage beneath a huge office building on Fifty-sixth Street. Convinced no one was following him, he drove down the steep ramp and stopped in front of the parking office. A skinny black teenager stood in the scuffed doorway. Ray flashed his badge.

"I need to park, but I want to do it myself," Ray said. "Are you cool with that?"

The black kid eyeballed the utilitarian Chevy, rolled his eyes, and shook his head.

"Smooth ride like you got there, I can see why." He put half a ticket on Ray's windshield and handed him the other. "Spaces down on the bottom level."

Everybody's a fucking comedian, Ray thought. Whatever happened to "The customer is always right"? He hit the gas and headed down the spiraling ramp.

He found a spot on the third level down. He parked, left the keys in the ignition, and got out. Instead of heading back up the ramp, he went deeper into the murky subbasement. There was a small, old elevator, a big dumbwaiter really, at the back wall that the carhops used to get back up to the office level. He knew about it because he'd chased down his first felony arrest, a purse snatcher, in this very garage six years ago. He could hear an engine approaching, and he stepped onto the little rubber platform and pushed the up button.

He hopped off the elevator at the top level, went to an unmarked door, and opened it. He entered the wide, empty corridor of the office building's basement and turned left, hurrying down the long hall. He came to another door, double-stepped up a flight of stairs into the building's lobby, and scooted out the revolving door to the street. He hurried in the rain across traffic-filled Fifty-fifth Street and walked through the loading docks for the post office that cut through to Fifty-fourth. The place where he'd rented the Chevy was on the corner of Third, and he looked up and down the block before he entered, smiling to himself in the vestibule. He was surprised that his own shadow was still attached to him after those moves.

It took twenty minutes to get a new rental car and another twenty to drive it back to the Bronx. He stopped beneath the El at the last station for the Number One subway line at Broadway and 242nd Street and looked around. He spotted Scully sitting at a park bench across the street with the bulging knapsack beneath him. Ray made a U-turn and pulled up.

Scully rose. He opened the door, threw the heavy bag into the passenger footwell, and dropped into the seat.

Ray offered a high five. Scully slapped it.

"Goddamn, my back's killin' me," he said.

"Let's see it," Ray said.

Scully unzipped the bag. Ray passed his right hand through the loose bills. A look of innocent, childish delight crossed his features.

Pay back that mob prick, he thought. Send Ma on a trip to the old sod. Set Carlita up someplace right. Still have some green left for the crap tables. This was it. The big score he'd always dreamed of, the one that would set things up, make things right.

"That's the nicest thing I've ever seen," he said.

It took another twenty-five minutes to get back to Hunts Point. Ray pulled over at a corner liquor store and came out with a bottle of champagne. They pulled up before Carlita's decimated building, and Scully grabbed the money-filled bag, and they got out.

They walked into the building and climbed the stairs.

"Pack your bags, sweetie," Ray said as he unlocked the apartment door.

He stopped dead still in the threshold. Scully bumped him from behind. The bottle of champagne fell and exploded on the floor.

CHAPTER TWENTY

THERE WERE MEN in the apartment. Two of them.

The first was a middle-aged Hispanic with bug eyes, holding Carlita by the back of her neck.

The other one was white with slicked silver hair and a business suit. He was sitting on the couch with the baby on his lap.

Ray went for his Glock at the small of his back but stopped when he heard a loud, slick clack a foot behind his head.

Correction, Ray thought. Three men. Something cold and hard touched the back of his head.

He put his hands in the air as he was shoved roughly against the wall. The Glock was taken from him. Scully was pushed to the wall beside him.

The door slammed shut. Locks turned.

"I fucking knew it," Ray heard Scully whisper under his breath.

Ray looked into the living room. The gentleman smiled. Ray thought of Brent with a quick touch of admiration. He hadn't thought the prick had it in him. The feeling soured as he watched the silver-haired man tickle the baby under his chin. Carlita moaned.

Ray glanced back quickly at the man holding the gun on him. A younger, thinner version of the frog-faced Hispanic with Carlita. The man frisked Ray fast and efficiently. He took the .38 out of his ankle holster and got the switchblade off the other leg. He took away his cuffs and his badge.

Then Scully was frisked and the money bag was ripped from him and tossed into the living room. It slid across the floor loudly and came to a stop next to the couch. The silver-haired man switched the baby to his other knee, took a peek in the bag, and nodded, satisfied. He leaned back, got comfortable.

"Hello, Ray."

"Who the fuck are you?" Ray said.

"C'mon, Ray. You're the man with the tape. Don't you recognize my voice?"

Ray squinted at him. Then his eyes widened.

"Oh, shit! You're Brent's bagman. Guest, right? I get it now. Hey, aren't you supposed to be busy burying bodies or something?"

Guest smiled.

"I got done a little early, Ray," he said. "Thought I might come by for a little chat. Nice moves today. You might even have gotten away if you weren't way out of your league. Now."

Guest straightened up. He jiggled the baby. Juan gurgled happily.

"Unfortunately, we don't get paid until everything is tidied up. Some questions still need answers. Like, are there any more copies of the tape? Where might they be? Who else is involved?"

"I understand we got some business to deal with here," Ray said. "But you're gonna find some hard fucking answers coming out of me unless you lay off the baby and the girl. If you know so much, then you know for a fact that girl don't even speak fuckin' English. She ain't involved."

"Yes, well. That's interesting," Guest said. "But I'm on a schedule here. I don't have the time to care."

A little muscle clenched hard in Ray's jaw.

"Then you better roll up your sleeves and put in for overtime, motherfucker. Because this is gonna be a long day."

Guest studied him for a moment, his lips pursed. A smirk came over his features. After a moment, he said something in quick, fluent Spanish and held up Juan.

"See," Guest said, looking at Ray. "I'm reasonable. Just don't make me regret it. If there's one thing I hate in this life, it's regret."

The man released Carlita. She went for her baby. Ray waited until she had the child in her arms. Then he wrapped his right fist around the handle of the small hidden knife at his belt buckle and took it out.

The thin man was bringing Scully's hand back to cuff him when Ray turned and punched him in the face. The blade sliced effortlessly through the man's cheek and clicked off his teeth. The Hispanic howled and fell back. Ray didn't even try for the TEC-9 the man had dropped, he just ripped out the wet knife.

Adrenaline was mainlining through him as he ran at the heavy one. The man managed to clear a nine-millimeter from his belt, but he didn't get the chance to fire it before Ray freight-trained into him. They fell to the floor. Ray lost the knife and jumped up. The fat man stayed where he was, gagging loudly. Ray looked and saw the blade buried in the man's Adam's apple. The man gagged again and blood spewed like a geyser.

There was a flutter behind him then. Ray jumped down. Rounds gouged plaster out of the wall. The front window blew out. Scully stood by the front door with the TEC-9 smoking in his hand. Guest was nowhere to be seen.

"He's in the kitchen!" Scully screamed.

Ray picked up the fat man's nine-millimeter and fired twice through the kitchen wall.

"Give me the gun!" Ray barked to Scully. "Take Carlita! Go!"

"But . . ."

"Go!"

Scully rushed over, handed him the pistol, and put an arm around Carlita. Ray shot down the hall next to the kitchen with the TEC-9. Scully got the door open, and they were gone.

The TEC-9 clicked empty, and Ray dropped it loudly to the floor. The fat one stumbled up moaning, and Ray shot him in the back.

Ray stood in the center of the room between the bagged money and the front door. The lady or the tiger, he thought crazily.

Fuck it.

He went for the bag.

He was at the money when he saw the man crouching out-side the fire escape window.

Ray brought the nine-millimeter up as the window crashed in. He felt something hot nick his side. He stopped and stood there.

Don't look!

He dropped his gun to the floor and lifted the bag. He stumbled across the floor bringing the bag up to his chest.

There was another shot. A heavy wet punch in his shoul-der.

So heavy, so goddamned heavy.

He was strong, though. Didn't they know that?

He turned and heaved the bag out the window that Scully had shot out. It hit the sill, sat there for a second, and then fell. There was another shot from behind him. Blood burst from his belly like a sneeze and sprayed the floor. His legs were gone, and he crashed to the wood.

He lay in his blood and thought about Scully sitting there on the bench waiting for him with the money after he'd conned him into the job.

Spend it, buddy. Every last fucking nickel. Get drunk like a motherfucker on me.

He heard a light footstep beside his head. He tried to turn toward it, put up his middle finger at least, but he couldn't. His heart had already stopped.

"GEE, THANKS FOR finally joining us," Guest said.

The mercenary, Ordell, stepped through the fire escape window into the apartment. He was a large man with a blond crew cut wearing an army coat and jeans. He unscrewed the silencer from the large silver revolver he held in his hand and put it in his pocket. He put the gun somewhere under his arm.

"Heard the shooting in the hall. Thought I'd make my way down from the roof."

"The money?" Guest asked.

"Landed in the street. Guy and the girl with the baby picked it up and drove off. I didn't have a shot."

Ordell looked down at two of the dead men.

"Ortiz brothers ain't looking so hot, huh?"

Guest shook his head in disappointment. He searched the cop. He found a cell phone and pocketed it.

"We got time to wipe things down?" Ordell said.

Before Guest could answer, sirens started up somewhere in the distance.

Guest frowned at him. He walked toward the door.

"Next time, when I tell you to wait for coffee," he said sternly, "listen to me."

CHAPTER TWENTY-ONE

I N THE CAB of the truck, Macklin flicked the heater to high and looked out upon black and empty Eleventh Avenue. It was three o'clock in the morning. Puckett played with the radio.

They were on another cable failure tonight, and they'd pinpointed it as being in the street, eleven feet north of the open manhole behind them. They were waiting for the dig crew to show up to rip open the street so they could access the cable to repair it.

Macklin still was feeling upbeat about his decision to turn in the tape. That afternoon before work, he'd felt so juiced that he'd managed to bundle up Christina and sit her in the yard as he raked leaves.

"Hey, check it out," Puckett said suddenly. He turned up the radio.

"Call now. Twenty-second caller for front-row Lionel Richie," the announcer said.

"Oh, you want to open up the station's line?" Macklin said. "Well . . . It is Lionel. 'Truly' live is definitely worth getting fired over."

"Or 'Dancing on the Ceiling'?" Puckett offered.

Macklin nodded with a grin.

"That shit brings the house down."

"C'mon, tell me some more crazy phone stories," Puckett said.

Macklin sat, considering all the things he'd seen and heard in the last six years working nights in the city. Of all of them, he realized, none came close in gravity to what he was actively attempting to pull off, and he was surprised to find that this distressed him. It seemed important that his new partner approve of him.

Wait, he thought. There was one thing he'd witnessed when he'd first started the job that made his transgressions pale in comparison. His face brightened.

"All right. You want to hear a story? I'll tell you something, okay? But this is extremely confidential. I never told this to anybody. Not even to my old partner, Jimmy, and he taught me this fucking job."

He looked over at Puckett, who seemed suitably solemn and impressed.

"Okay," Macklin said. "The first week I got this job, there was a mistake and they sent me out to Brooklyn. To Bensonhurst. You ever heard of it?"

"Italian?" Puckett said.

Macklin nodded.

"You better believe it. Anyway, I'm the new guy, so they

stick me on nights, right? I'm partnered up with this Irish lunatic, guy from Queens named Danny Kelly. This guy was old-school phone company: Vietnam vet, drug addict, drunk. His foreman fucked up the overtime on his check one time, and he told him he'd killed men in Southeast Asia for less than minimum wage and that it wouldn't take anything at all to do it over time-and-a-half. They sent him to the drunk farm fifteen times or some shit. A record he was proud of. Anyway, my luck, I get put with this nut, and a week goes by and one night we're in the basement of some building doing a throw. We're sitting around—waiting for some more cable to be delivered—with another team. Two old-timers. They're both drinking with Kelly and I'm hiding in the corner, afraid I'm gonna get fired. There was an open cable along the wall, and Kelly hops up and starts fuckin' around with a dial set.

"'Hey, check this out,'" he says after a minute, and puts it on speaker.

"'You better listen up, you lying, cheating whore,' this Italian guy is yelling. 'Because soon as I get outta here, you're goin' in a hole!' Then this lady says, 'Marco, you know I wouldn't do you that way, baby.' 'My brother seen you, bitch,' this guy says. And blah-blah-blah, 'as soon as I get out of C-block, you're dead!'"

"A mobster?" Puckett said.

"I guess so," Macklin said. "Anyway, she's going, 'You're crazy. I love you, sweetie, and you know your brother's a drunk and I'll wait for you for as long as it takes.' And then Kelly, this fuckin' nut, clicks onto the line and says, 'Hey, baby. What's takin' you so long? Come back to bed.' And then he clips off the line."

Puckett's eyes went wide.

"No!" he said.

Macklin nodded.

"We just sat there, stunned, looking up at Kelly, who's laughing his ass off.

"'You know what you did, Danny?' one of the old-timers says. 'You just got that girl killed.' And Kelly just shrugged his shoulders and said, 'There any beers left?'"

"Get the fuck outta here!"

Macklin looked off down the bleak, dark roadway.

See, he wasn't so bad, he assured himself.

That motherfucker Kelly was way worse.

"Like I said, I don't ever want to hear that story back," Macklin said gravely. "You got me?"

"No problem," Puckett said, following his gaze.

They sat in silence. Macklin peered at Puckett.

"You want to hear another one?" he said.

"That's okay," said Puckett. "I'm fine."

Half an hour later, the dig crew showed. Four men in a large, open-bedded work truck with another driving a back-hoe. Macklin got out of the truck to meet them. He'd worked with this same crew before, and the backhoe driver called out to him as he came over.

"Hey, Seany. How you doin'?" he said, stepping down and shaking his hand. "Whatdaya got for us tonight?"

He was a stocky, older man, with a thick Italian accent, named Tony. He wore short sleeves despite the cold. Most of the road guys were Italians. They said you had to speak Sicilian in order to get on.

"We're looking at eleven feet north of the duct," Macklin said.

"Top bank?" Tony asked.

"Yeah, but second row down, west."

Tony nodded as they walked toward the hole. He squatted on his heels beside their open manhole and squinted at the patched street before him, like a golfer reading a putt. Then he went under the barrier tape and climbed down into the hole and came back up a moment later. One of the men handed Tony an orange spray can, and he stepped off a distance north of the hole and sprayed out a neat rectangle.

"Why don' you go get outta the cold for a while, Sean?" Tony said. "Gonna take two hours at least. I beep ya."

Macklin gave him his number and stepped into the truck with Puckett. They drove to the nearest central office. There were some chairs and a desk inside the rarely used second-floor frame, and they went in past the security guard and took the elevator up.

Macklin lay down on the polished floor in front of the frame and closed his eyes.

"Gonna be a while," he said. "I'm gonna crash until Tony beeps us."

"Okay, I'm gonna get something to eat," Puckett said. "You want something?"

"Nah, I'm all right," Macklin said.

He lay with his eyes closed, listening to the fading sound of Puckett's footsteps. The frame door opened and closed, and then there was just the hum of the fluorescent lights.

Macklin tried to rest, but he couldn't. He should call Ray, he thought. It'd been a while. Maybe he'd made some progress with the tape. He took a dial set out of his bag beside him and clipped it onto a line on the frame beside where he lay. He knew you weren't supposed to use customer lines for personal calls, but what are you gonna do? Eavesdropping and insider trading weren't exactly in the employee work code manual either. He dialed his brother's number.

It picked up on the second ring.

"Hey, Ray. It's Sean. What's up?" Macklin said.

Silence.

"Ray?"

"What's up?" a voice said smoothly.

It wasn't Ray's.

"Who's this? Where's Ray?"

"He's incapacitated at the moment. Can I take a message?"

Incapacitated? Macklin thought.

"That's all right," he said after a second. "I'll call back."

Macklin hung up and lay the dial set down beside his head. What the fuck was that all about? Did he call the wrong number? He jumped when the dial set rang a second later, a loud piercing purr in the empty, cavernous room. Macklin answered it without thinking.

"Why, hello there, Sean," said the voice that he'd just spoken to. The voice was confident now, mocking.

"It's me, Ray."

"Huh?" Macklin got out.

"Huh?" the voice mimicked loudly.

Macklin just yanked the dial set back hard, unclipping its leads off the frame, disconnecting the call.

What the fuck was that about?

Ray's partner must have answered his phone and then hit *69 to call back and fuck with him, Macklin rationalized.

Fuckin' cops, he thought. They were all nuts.

Macklin looked down the long corridor of the frame at

wires upon wires upon wires. He took a breath and laid his head back down on the floor. He closed his eyes, listening to the hum.

I'll just give Ray a call tomorrow, he thought.

DRESSED ALL IN black, Guest stood in the unfamiliar kitchen, letting his eyes adjust to the darkness. He took his knapsack off his back, unzipped it, and removed a black leather bag. It was a doctor's bag, but the instruments it held had never been used for healing.

Half an hour earlier in his hotel room, the phone that he'd taken off the cop's body had rung. Although he hadn't convinced the caller that he was the cop, he had been able to jot down the number that appeared in the caller ID screen. Because of the lateness of the call and the party's suspicious behavior, Guest had made the decision that the caller had something to do with the shakedown.

He'd called the number back, but the man had hung up. Ten minutes later, he'd called back again. It rang four times, and then a machine picked it up.

"Hi. You've reached the home of Frank Hale. I can't come to the phone right now but . . ."

He'd found a Frank Hale at 221 East Thirty-third Street in the Manhattan white pages listed with the same number he'd gotten from the cell phone. It'd taken fifteen minutes for Ordell to arrive and drive him to Hale's building and another five to pick the locks.

Guest closed his eyes and listened. Breathing, faint and steady, came from a room off to the left. He stepped quietly toward it. Through the door, Guest could make out a sleeping form in the bed. He removed a hypodermic needle from his bag. Without turning on the light, he walked to the sleeping man and stabbed the needle into his shoulder.

Guest flicked on the lights. This man was bald and over-weight. He checked his pulse, then took a penlight out of the bag and checked his pupils.

"Good," he said.

He needed answers right away this time. No more non-sense after what the cop had pulled. He cleared off a space on the desk near the bed. After he had everything arranged, he took out a small radio.

"Okay, Ordell," he whispered into it. "Come on up."

CHAPTER TWENTY-TWO

SCULLY WALKED ACROSS the grease-stained cement into the gas station Snack Mart and asked the clerk for twenty dollars on pump two. There was a display of Heineken twelve-packs beside where he stood waiting. When the clerk came back, Scully had the beer up on the counter. He paid for everything with a hundred, took his change and beer, and went back to his car.

He put the beer in the well of the front seat. He leaned against the side of the car, looking out on the highway as the tank filled, trucks and cars whipping past in the gray morning light.

He was in Delaware now. He'd been driving ever since he'd left Carlita and Juan in the hotel beside the George Washington Bridge the night before. They'd both been sleeping, and he'd put fifty thousand dollars in Carlita's bag and left. The rest of the money was in the trunk now, under the spare.

The pump clicked, and he replaced the nozzle. He got back in the car and pulled out onto the road.

He'd have to dump the car soon enough, he knew. It was registered in Ray's name, and they'd be looking for it before long. He'd decided on Florida as his destination. He could stop in Baltimore and get a plane, or better yet, catch an Amtrak. They had bars on trains, didn't they? That's exactly what he needed, a traveling bar.

Scully remembered the money sitting like a Christmas present out on the sidewalk. He'd circled the block, and when he came back around, he saw Guest in the lobby. He knew it meant that Ray was dead, and he'd peeled out of there. He hadn't stopped until they were out of the city altogether. He got them a room in a Fort Lee hotel, but an hour later, he was back out on the road alone. The way things had been avalanching, abandoning the woman and baby was the nicest thing he could think to do.

Scully looked at the beers beside him. Not now, he thought. With his luck, he'd take a sip and look up to find a state trooper next to him. He'd pull over and get a room soon enough. Get drunk and sleep. Get a train in the evening. He had money now, the open road, no responsibilities. Wasn't this what he'd always wanted?

He could see Ray again, taking people down, telling him to get Carlita out of there. See him firing down the hall as they ran out, leaving him there to die.

Scully took a breath and scanned the gray horizon.

CHAPTER TWENTY-THREE

THERE WAS LITTLE traffic on the parkway heading out of the city in the morning. Macklin got home quickly. He pulled into the driveway beside the nurse's car and shut the engine. As he walked to the front door, he looked out at the new carpet of leaves on the front lawn that had replaced the ones he'd raked up the day before.

Story of my life, he thought.

Rose was walking Christina out of the bathroom when he came in.

"Morning," he said.

Christina stood, looking blankly at the floor. The nurse at her elbow smiled.

"Morning, Mr. Macklin."

He went to the back room where he slept during the day

and sat on the couch. He was taking off his boots when the phone rang. They rarely got calls, and he was going to let it go as a solicitor when he thought of his brother. He reached over to the small table and lifted the receiver off the hook.

"Yeah?"

"Sean?"

It was his mother. *His mother?*

"Ma?"

"Sean," she said. There was emotion in her usually stern voice. Pain. Something was definitely wrong.

"Ma, what is it? What?"

"It's Raymond. There was . . ." she paused, sobbing. "There was a shooting."

Macklin's mouth fell open.

"No!" he said.

"He was off duty," his mother said. "They said . . ."

Dear God, no. Ray. Please not Ray.

"Where'd they take him?"

"No. He's . . ."

She sobbed.

"They found him this morning."

Macklin let his head fall against the wall. He could feel something dark and cold spill suddenly into his blood.

"No," he said.

"Oh, Sean," his mother said.

"Who did it? What happened? Did they catch anyone?"

"No, the police are here now."

"I'm on my way," he said.

She hung up. Macklin closed his eyes tight, still holding the receiver to his ear. He ignored the operator's polite plea for him to put it down. Only when the amplified electronic blast shot through his skull for a full minute did he do as asked. He lifted the plastic phone off the table and flung it across the room. It rang like a bell off the wall.

He came out and told Rose what had happened, and she looked at him in pity and said she would cover for him. He got back in the car and drove. The sun was coming up now, a hazy circle of white, flickering behind the black bars of the leafless, roadside trees. He turned off the highway and onto his old block a little less than an hour later. There was a Gran Fury and a blue-and-white police cruiser parked in front of the house he'd grown up in, and he pulled to a stop behind them and got out.

His mother came to the door with tears in her eyes. He put his arms around her wiry frame, and she clung to him desperately for a brief second. Cops filled the small kitchen, drinking tea. Two uniforms and two plainclothes, radios squawking. One of the plainclothes looked up at him solemnly from the table. He rose and extended a hand.

"Sean?" he said.

Macklin glared.

"What happened?" he said.

The detective took him by the arm.

"Come outside for a smoke."

They stepped out onto the deck that overlooked the tiny backyard. The detective took cigarettes out.

"What happened to my brother?" Macklin said.

The detective looked off over the backyard fence.

"Two o'clock yesterday afternoon, a shots fired came in at your brother's precinct. When police got to the scene, they found your brother dead. Shot three times. He was off-duty at the time. There was an IAD file on your brother. Did you know that?"

Macklin looked at him.

"How the fuck would I know that?"

"You and Ray close?"

"Yes. No. I don't know."

"Well, there's speculation that he was involved with some corruption. As far as that goes, I wouldn't know, but the way he was found, it has the earmark of a drug hit."

Macklin grasped the iron railing. It was cold, burning. He squeezed it hard.

"No," he said. "That's bullshit. Not Ray."

"Is there anything you can tell me that might help us find out what happened? Anything he might have said to you?"

Macklin shook his head.

"Nothing," he said. He looked at the detective. "Drugs?"

The detective shrugged. He exhaled smoke from his nose. He was about to flick his cigarette across the yard, but then thought better of it. He put it out on the sole of his shoe and then put the butt in the pocket of his suit coat.

"It coulda been. We're gonna to do our best to paint things the right way. Even if this was a little wrong, your brother was a good cop, as far as I can see. Plus, your father was very well-respected in the force and there are still people around who haven't forgotten that. But, this is an election year, so I can't tell you what's going to happen in the papers."

The papers, Macklin thought. He shook his head. The detective put a hand on his shoulder.

"Listen, your mother needs someone. Can you take time off work?"

"Uh-huh."

The detective took out a card.

"This is a PBA lawyer. He'll help you take care of the arrangements. Listen, I don't give a fuck what the papers or the brass say. Ray was one of us. We're going to do everything we can to find out who did this to him and to protect his memory. You have my word on that."

Macklin took the card. He nodded. The detective opened the back door and stood in it.

"Take care of your mother," he said.

Macklin stood on the deck. Cold wind bent the yellowed stubble of grass in the tiny yard.

Drugs, he thought. Was that possible? Ray? He knew Ray liked to gamble. Maybe it had something to do with that. There was no way for him to know. They'd grown apart. One meeting at a diner in a year didn't mean shit.

He searched the yard where they'd tackled each other playing football, and the other dusty, cement backyards they'd run through growing up.

He wiped his wet eyes before he went back in the house. His mother was leading the police officers out the front door.

"They said the papers would call," she said when she came back in.

"I'll take care of that, Ma. Did Ray say anything to you? Was he acting funny?"

His mother looked at him. She seemed puzzled suddenly as to why he was there. She shook her head slowly, to answer his question or perhaps a sad one she'd asked herself, he didn't know. Then she walked into the kitchen. After a second, he heard the tap go on and the banging of plates. He left her to herself, walked to the rear of the house, and opened his old bedroom door.

The room was pretty much the same except there weren't

any bunk beds. The Yankee posters had been taken down, but there was still a signed ball on the dresser. He sat down on the bed. He remembered lying in the dark before falling asleep when they were kids, talking, joking. That his brother could be dead seemed unreal. Ray had looked so good at the diner. So healthy and upbeat. Macklin looked up at his brother's stereo system, and it was only then that he remembered the tape. He stood suddenly.

Fuck! The tape! he thought. Jesus Christ, if somebody found the tape he was doomed, done for. He'd lose his job. Where would Ray have put it? He stood and opened his brother's top dresser drawer. There among his socks and underwear were metal objects. Weapons, folding knives and brass knuckles and saps. Behind them were cardboard boxes of bullets of various calibers. He sifted among everything, but he couldn't find the tape.

He was looking in the closet when the doorbell rang. He thought it might be a reporter already, and he left the room and went to the door to curse him out. Two men in neat suits were standing on the porch when he opened it. One of them slid out a black billfold and flipped it open.

"FBI," it read.

Oh, fuck, Macklin thought.

"Is this the home of Raymond Macklin?" the older of them said. He had silver hair and cold, piercing eyes that he leveled steadily at Macklin. The other agent was younger and larger and wore a crew cut and a mean smile.

"Yeah?" Macklin said, putting some belligerence in his tone.

"Who are you, please?"

"I'm his brother," Macklin said.

The agents exchanged looks.

"Your brother was the subject of a federal investigation. We'd like to ask you some questions. May we come in?"

Macklin stepped out of the doorway and onto the concrete stoop, closing the door behind him.

"No, you may not come in. My mother just heard her son is dead. We're a little busy now."

"Well, I'm afraid that's not good enough, Sean," the silver-haired agent said, glancing again at his still silent partner.

What the fuck?

"It is Sean, isn't it?"

Macklin stared from one to the other, a feeling of dread beginning to undercut his anger.

"What do you want?"

"There are just a few issues that need clearing up," the lead agent said. "We'd like you to come with us to answer some questions."

Issues? Macklin thought crazily.

They know about the tape.

Macklin had to stop himself from swallowing.

Maybe not everything, he thought, but they know. What the fuck to do? Play stupid.

"What issues?"

The silver-haired agent smirked at him wearily, like a parent disappointed with a lying child. He gestured toward the car.

"We just need an hour of your time," the agent said. He opened the lapel of his jacket slightly to show handcuffs and a black, holstered automatic at his belt.

"Unless you want us to play hardball right now, Sean. It's up to you."

Fuck me, Macklin thought, panicked. Things were moving way too fast.

If he turned them down, would they arrest him? He'd have to go. How would he feel if he were innocent? Reluctant, he figured, grudging.

Macklin rolled his eyes and shook his head as if pissed. He hoped they were buying it.

"All right. I'll put up with one hour of your bullshit, if you're gonna take me in otherwise. But I can't leave my mom alone any longer than that."

He went back inside. His mother was scrubbing viciously at the table when he walked into the kitchen. When he told her he'd be back in a little while, she didn't even turn around.

He came back outside, and the two agents walked down the stairs behind him. They opened the back door of the blue Crown Victoria at the curb and escorted him in. They got on the Major Deegan Expressway south for the city. Macklin sat, looking out at the bleak, passing roadway trying to look calm, trying to quell the increasing waves of nervousness that crashed in his belly.

Of all the luck, he thought. Not only did Ray have to die, he had to die with the illegal tape that he'd given him on him. Why hadn't the NYPD detective mentioned anything? Had he been trying to trick him?

Ray, Macklin thought, holding his head in his hands. He couldn't believe his brother was dead.

"Cigarette?"

Macklin turned. The younger agent was offering a smoke from the passenger seat. It was the first time the man had spoken. There was a Southern twang to his voice.

Macklin shook his head.

They pulled off at an exit and crossed a rusting steel beam bridge into Manhattan.

They drove through Harlem. After a while, they got on Central Park West. The silver-haired agent was driving. Macklin exchanged a glance with him in the rearview mirror.

"You said an hour," Macklin said. "Where the hell are we going?"

"Don't worry," the agent said. "We're just about there."

They drove in silence. When the Southern agent lit a cigarette, the snap and click of his lighter seemed earsplitting. Macklin could just make out the raised insignia on the lighter: US NAVY SEALS.

They'd hit some traffic in the Seventies when the silver-haired agent started whistling. Macklin had his head down, still trying desperately to calm himself. It infuriated him that the agent could be so cool.

Then the old song the agent was whistling suddenly registered.

He looked up and watched the man's pursed lips in the mirror. He listened, almost hearing the words.

The summer wind came blowing in from across the sea.

Everything came together in quick succession.

The guy who'd answered his brother's cell phone the night before, Ray's sudden death, the professional way in which he'd been killed.

A series of switches thrown, a circuit completed.

Guest.

Guest noticed Macklin watching him.

"You feeling all right?" he said.

Macklin listened intently without taking his eyes away.

You feeling all right? Macklin thought.

There's been an incident, Mr. Brent. Is this line secure?

The inflection, the tone.

No doubt.

It was him.

"Yeah," Macklin forced himself to say. His mouth was suddenly without saliva, his throat raw.

"Conscience bothering you?" the Southern agent said. He began to guffaw.

Macklin couldn't take his eyes away from Guest's in the rearview. Cold, empty, laughing at him.

Guest had come up from Central America after covering up the conspiracy, Macklin realized. He'd found out that Ray had the tape somehow, and he'd killed him for it. Guest had gotten Ray's address and had come by after the cops left to tie up loose ends. Macklin was one of those loose ends.

Macklin looked down.

They were no FBI agents. They were killers.

Jesus Christ, Macklin thought in horror. He'd gotten his own brother killed.

No, he couldn't think of that now. There was no time. This FBI charade would be over in a minute and guns would be drawn. He forced himself to think.

They hadn't frisked him at least. He still had his splicer's knife and shears on his belt. He slipped the steel shears out furtively and held them down by his leg. Hardly a weapon at all, but he needed out of this car.

Wait, he thought for a second. What if these two really were agents and he tried something? Where the fuck would he be then? He'd been up all night and maybe the shock of everything was making him paranoid. He thought hard. Okay, that song was no coincidence. It was Guest. But did Guest being here now definitely mean the man had killed his brother? Maybe it was just a coincidence and he only wanted to question him. There was one way to find things out for certain.

Macklin looked up at the rearview. Guest was busy watching the road. With his shears still in his hand, Macklin reached slowly into his jacket pocket and felt for his cell phone. He turned it on with his thumb, quietly dialed his brother's cell phone number and waited.

He took a breath.

"Maybe I will take that smoke after all," he said to the Southerner.

Macklin waited for the man to retrieve the cigarettes. As the Southerner turned over the front seat toward him, Macklin ran his thumb down the slightly raised plastic buttons of the phone in his pocket and pressed down *send*.

There was a moment of complete silence, a pure second that hovered between two beats of Macklin's heart. Then the cell phone Guest had picked off his brother's dead body bleated loudly from somewhere within Guest's jacket, and Macklin moved.

The Southerner wasn't paying attention as he offered the cigarette, so he didn't catch the rage that reared suddenly in Macklin's eyes with the phone's ring. Macklin didn't take the cigarette that dangled from between the man's thick fingers, but he did grab his wrist. He brought his shears up and caught the Southerner's thumb between their sharp twin blades and squeezed.

The man screamed. The shears cut through the flesh easily, but jammed at the bone. Macklin yelled and bore down savagely with his work-hardened hands on the thumb of this cocksucker who'd murdered his brother, and the blades snipped through bone at the first joint and the thumb tip flew.

The Southerner was convulsing. Blood squirted over the seats and on the dashboard and windows. His brother's cell phone chirped on. Guest brought the car into a skid as Macklin got the rear door open. He rolled out as it was still moving and went flying, sliding over the asphalt. Then he was up and running across the street as horns blared. Central Park was right there, and as he dove over the low wall, something gouged out a chunk of the dark stone by his hand. Although he hadn't heard anything, he didn't need to turn to know he was being shot at. There was a drop of six feet, but he didn't even feel it. He was too busy running, breath ragged in his lungs, heading up the slope for the trees. His blood-covered shears were still in his hand, he noted crazily, and he slid them back into their sheath as he ran.

CHAPTER TWENTY-FOUR

GUEST WENT TO fire again, but his target had dropped out of sight.

He made a screeching U-turn beside the park, stopped the car, and got out. Ordell held his bloody hand in against his body, cursing. The look of agony in the man's face was remarkable. Guest ignored it. He reached in and grabbed one of the radios, tossing the other at Ordell.

"Stay in the car. Listen to my instructions," Guest yelled as he bolted.

The coattails of Guest's suit sailed up as he vaulted over the wall.

TIRED AND WHEEZING, Macklin had reached the far side of the Sheep Meadow the first time he turned around. He did so just in time to catch sight of a man in a business suit hurdle the distant fence without breaking his surprisingly fast stride. Macklin turned and sprinted, terror giving him new wind.

He chanced a second glance back after he crossed Fifth Avenue a minute later. Guest was landing gracefully on his black-shoed feet from the wall across the wide avenue. Macklin was close enough to see that the man had hardly built up a sweat.

Guest had closed the distance to half a block by the time Macklin got to the subway entrance outside of Bloomingdale's. Macklin took the steep, stained steps down two at a time. The token clerk squawked protest out of his loudspeakers as Macklin hopped the turnstile. There was no train at the platform, so he ran for the stairs to the lower-level train. A train was pulling in as he hit the platform, and he ran down to the end and waited for the doors to open, his heart hammering. When they finally opened, he stepped on and sat down, sweating and hacking and watching the stairs. The doors bonged their two notes and began to shut, but opened suddenly again.

"Hey, knuckleheads in the front, stop holding the door," the conductor said over the speaker.

They bonged again and began to shut. In the distance, Macklin saw Guest burst onto the platform, and the doors opened. Then they closed and the train shuddered to life and began to move.

No! Macklin thought.

Guest was on the train.

Macklin was in the front car, so there was no getting any farther away from where Guest had embarked, about five cars back. Macklin knew the front door on the train was kept locked, so he stepped quickly down the car to the opposite door. He slid it open, stood in the loud space between the cars, and let it crash closed. Looking through the scratched glass into the next car, he kept his eyes on the window at the far end of the second car, waiting to catch any glimpse of Guest. His only hope was for Guest to start his search at the rear cars of the train first. By the time he realized his mistake, the train would be at the next station and Macklin could try to lose him there. The train went into a screaming curve, and Macklin had to watch his feet so they didn't get crushed as the two cars began to separate and tap back. When it straightened out, he looked up to see Guest opening the door at the opposite end of the second car.

Macklin didn't think that Guest would fire across a crowded subway car, but he was wrong. Before the door had closed behind him, Guest had his black automatic out and up and was sighting down it. Macklin threw himself back as three shots crashed in a tight pattern through the glass where his face had been. There were muffled screams from the car, and staying low, Macklin backed and opened the door to the front car and threw himself in. Macklin pulled himself up panicking, looking around. He spotted the emergency brake on the wall above the door, and he reached up and opened its steel box. A siren began to go off, and he grasped the red handle and yanked it down.

There was a scream of metal. Macklin was thrown forward against the door. Back through the glass, he saw Guest lose his feet and sail forward into a pole and go down. The train was slowing. Macklin cursed himself for not waiting until Guest came through the door to pull the brake because now the train would just be stuck in the tunnel and Guest would regain his feet and come after him. He looked through the front window of the car to the distant glow of the next station up the tunnel. The train continued to skid, but it wasn't going to be enough. When they came to a complete stop, Macklin saw that though the whole car hadn't cleared the station's platform, half of the very first front door had, and he ran for it. He wasn't about to wait for the driver to open the door, so he just pulled himself up on two hanging metal straps and kicked with his heavy work boots. The glass starred, and he swung back and double-kicked again. This time the glass popped out in a single piece onto the cement platform with a crash, and he jumped out after it.

The train driver was hanging out the window as Macklin ran past him up the station.

"Get your ass back here!" the driver boomed.

Macklin didn't even turn around.

It was the Forty-second Street Station, and he zigzagged quickly through the large crowd. He passed through the turnstile at a run. There was a wide corridor beyond it and he sped down it. After a minute, he entered Grand Central Station. There were a lot of cops standing around, and he slowed his pace over the white stone tiles. He couldn't ask for help because of the tape. He turned up the ramp for the Forty-second Street exit, got to the door, and stepped out.

New York City seemed like such a huge, easy place to hide in until you were being chased in it. He thought to use his company ID to get into one of the office buildings and hide in the basement phone room, but then he remembered that Guest's FBI badge could probably get him in anywhere as well. When he looked up, he saw the Park Avenue Viaduct, and he crossed the street.

Something made him glance back at Grand Central before he turned the corner.

Impossible.

Guest was standing on the balls of his feet in front of the doors from which he'd just emerged. Macklin watched him smile and raise a finger and shake it at him. Macklin stood, rooted. Guest would catch him anyway, so he might as well stay here and have it done with. Then the spell broke and he bolted into a run.

The recessed door to the telephone vault was only fifty feet up the block, but he'd have to get it open before Guest crossed the street. He already had his key out when he got to it. He knew he'd have one, seamless shot, and he just took a breath and let his fingers slide the key into the door and unlock it. Then he opened the door slightly, jumped in through the crack, and pulled it shut.

He leaned back against the inside of the door wheezing silently, his heart bursting. Sweat seemed to pour from every inch of his body. Dust from the chamber clung to his face, the back of his neck. There was no way to know what Guest was doing out on the sidewalk, but after five minutes, the door hadn't been tried.

It was an hour later the next time he moved. His clothes were soaked with sweat, and he began to feel cold. It was only then that he allowed the full weight of it all to crash down upon him.

Ray, he thought.

Macklin sank to his knees in the dust of the hole beneath the road and began to sob.

"HEY! HEY, YOU!"

Guest turned. A policeman was running up the block toward him.

"Where the fuck are you!" Guest called into his radio as he began moving.

"HERE!" Ordell yelled, screeching to a stop across the street.

Guest ran over and got in, and Ordell floored it. They ran two red lights and made a right.

"You lost him?" Ordell said. "Don't tell me you lost him."

"For the moment," Guest said, taking out a piece of paper and a pen. He took out a cell phone and began to dial.

"Who you calling? Brent?"

"Not right now," Guest said. "I got the brother's plate number back at the cop's house. I'm gonna get someone to run it for me."

Guest spoke into the phone, listened, and wrote something down. He hung up.

"Back to the cop's house?" Ordell asked

Guest looked at the paper.

"No, farther north. Brother Sean's got himself a house up in Duchess County."

"Please have a family," Ordell said, shifting his injured hand and squinting out the windshield. "Please."

CHAPTER TWENTY-FIVE

MACKLIN WIPED HIS eyes finally and raised himself up in the dark. He remembered the bag he'd left here in the vault. He felt his way along the cold stone walls. He found the vault door and fit the key into the lock by feel and opened it up. He banged his head three times on cable hangers before he found the bag. He unzipped it, retrieved his flashlight, and switched it on. He sunk to the floor, holding it before him.

He remembered his mother then. He had to warn her. He took a dial set out of the bag and stood. With a cable hanger he found on the floor, he knocked off the locking bars to a splice case and slid off its shell. He clipped through some lines until he found dial tone, and he dialed his mother's number. When she answered, he told her not to let anybody in the house and to call the detective who had been there that morning and tell him she was feeling afraid for her life and ask him to send a squad car over. She told him that he was crazy, but he kept telling her to do it until she promised, and then he hung up.

Okay, he thought.

The jig was up. Guest knew that he was responsible for the tape and was out there right now looking for him. It wasn't like he could go to the cops. What he'd have to do was get scarce. He had some vacation time coming. He'd give it another hour, and then he'd sneak out of here, go to the bank, and get a train home from Grand Central to get Christina. Any plans after that, he'd just have to figure it out.

He sat down and looked up at the darkened ceiling of the vault. He thought of the man whom he'd just cut. He hoped the fucker bled to death. His only regret was that he didn't have time to stick his shears in Guest's ear. Damn, that cocksucker was fast. And the balls it took to shoot in the subway car! No hesitation. After Guest blew him away, he would've just taken out that fake FBI badge and bluffed until he could get away. It was sheer luck that Macklin was still alive.

Well, I got one of them, Ray, he thought.

But what about that smiling prick, Brent? That son of a bitch had started this whole thing and nothing would happen to him. He'd have his merger and he'd make millions.

Macklin stood slowly, a wild thought coming to him. He lifted his knapsack of telephone equipment and picked up the flashlight.

Maybe he could rectify that.

Macklin walked quickly through the corridors until he reached Brent's cable. He taped the flashlight to a case above, pointing it down to where he'd be working. He opened up the splice case and culled out Brent's line. He clipped his dial set on it and heard dial tone. He hit some numbers and the phone company's familiar computer voice began reciting Brent's number. He disengaged.

Using the dial set, he began to search through the lines that ran alongside Brent's. With the first one he found dial tone on, he took out his shears, cut it, and stripped back its insulation. Then he cut Brent's line, stripped back its insulation, and twisted its copper to the other line. Then he clipped his dial set to the other side of Brent's line and waited for it to ring.

Brent's line would no longer ring in his office, but at the dial set before him. He'd given Brent another line to remove any suspicion.

Macklin thought of Brent's voice from the tape, smooth and deep, vaguely intelligent-sounding, like a news anchor's.

"Hello, Brent here," he practiced in the dark. "Brent here. Hello?"

The phone rang for the first time less than a minute later. Macklin picked it up on its second ring.

"Brent," he said.

"Robert? Ted. How are you?"

Ted ? Macklin thought.

"Fine, Ted, and you?" Macklin said.

"Well, I'm real interested in your progress. Do you think you'll have that offer ready?"

Offer, Macklin thought. He thought about the tape and the deal. Ted was Ted Phillips, the head of Allied, and he wanted to know about the progress on the merger.

"Well, um . . ."

"What is it, Robert? You sound funny this morning."

Macklin thought quickly. Hadn't Brent told his lawyer that he didn't want to do a hostile merger? Well, anything Brent didn't want to do was a good thing. Maybe he could fuck things up in that direction. He thought of the things Speed had said.

"I'll just come out and say it. My board wants to go hostile. I told them it was just plain wrong, Ted, that we had a deal, but . . ."

"What?" Phillips said. His voice seemed to raise a full octave. "Are you sure?"

"Positive, Ted. Oh, and beware of First Investment and that Speed Angstrom. They're the ones handling the whole thing. Good Luck."

"But . . ." Ted said.

Macklin hung up.

Had Ted fallen for it? He'd confused him at least, and maybe just that would fuck things up. Whatever, Macklin thought. It beat doing nothing.

The phone rang again. How many calls does this cocksucker get a day? Macklin thought, picking it up.

"Robert Brent," Macklin said. He smiled to himself. He'd nailed Brent's tone perfectly this time.

"Yes, Mr. Brent. This is Felicia Wood from Sterling Aviation. Mitch Gabriel informed me you're in the market for an aircraft?"

"That's right," Macklin said, going along with her.

"Well, what exactly are your needs, and I'll see if we can accommodate."

"Well, Felicia. We need something very, very large and very, very luxurious. We're sending our sales force to Egypt next month, and we want to fly them on our own company jet."

"Wow! A month. That might be a crunch. How many passengers are you talking about?"

"One hundred and seventeen."

"Hmm. To Egypt, too. That means you need transcontinental capability. We have a refurbished seven-twenty-seven you might be interested in. It belonged to the royal family of Abu Dhabi. It's quite elegant."

"I'll take it," Macklin said.

"Are you serious?"

"Oh, I'm always serious, Ms. Wood. Draw up a detailed report with the costs to satisfy the accountants. I tell you right now, though, it sounds exactly like what we're looking for. I must go now. Thank you," he said, and hung up.

Macklin checked his watch. He had time to answer one more phone call. Then he had to get out his money and go home and get his wife.

CHAPTER
TWENTY-SIX

BRENT AWOKE TIRED. He'd been in a merger strategy session the night before that had run until midnight. The only remaining item to be negotiated now was the tender offer. Chemtech would be taking on Allied, so they had to come up with a fair offer to buy out the controlling interest of Allied's stock. Sam had come up with a cash-stock swap that seemed to serve the interests of all parties involved, but they'd have to take another quick look at it. They would present it for Allied's approval today at a meeting scheduled for one P.M. at his office.

He looked at the clock. Nine-thirty. Time to get his lazy ass out of bed. He sat up. He gazed admiringly at Martine lying naked and asleep in the bed beside him. Hers could stay right where it was.

He was coming out of the shower when the phone rang. He picked it up.

"Brent here."

"Robert, thank God I caught you. Have you seen the board this morning?"

It was Speed.

"No," Brent said warily. "What is it?"

"Allied," Speed said. "There's been play ever since the bell rang. Someone is scooping up Allied stock like mad."

"Who? What?"

"I don't know who, but I was hoping it was you, because when I called Allied, they said they wouldn't talk to me."

"Wouldn't talk to you? What the hell is going on?"

"If I had to guess, it's either someone coming in trying to take the company or Allied's shoring itself up for an attack. Driving up its own price to squelch our deal."

Good God! Now what?

"But I spoke to Phillips last night," Brent said. "We're ready to move."

"Well, something happened, Robert. Maybe you could call Phillips and try to find out."

"Okay," Brent said. "I'll call you back."

Still in his towel, he hung up and dialed Phillips.

His secretary answered. What was her name? Mary.

"Mary, it's Robert Brent here. I have to talk to Ted."

"Please hold," she said coldly.

She was usually extremely warm. What was going on?

"Mr. Phillips is unavailable at this time. Would you like to leave a message?"

"Unavailable! What in good goddamn is going on? This is Robert Brent."

"I know who this is," the secretary said. "Would you like to leave a message?"

"Yeah. Ask him why he isn't taking my calls."

Brent slammed the phone down and dialed his office.

"Brent here," came a voice.

Brent? What!

"Who is this?" Brent asked.

"Oh, hey, it's you, Brent. How you doing?" the voice said.

"Who are you? What are you doing at my office?"

"I'm you, Brent. At least for today, I am. Go back to bed. I'll take care of everything."

Brent thought he might pass out. He was going crazy. That's what it was.

"Who are you?" he called out.

"I'm the Ghost of Christmas Yet to Come, motherfucker. And I'm coming for you, Brent. Me and all the other ghosts you made down in El Salvador."

"Stop! Just stop it!"

"See you soon."

The line went dead.

Brent quickly called back his office. The line was busy. He tried it again and it rang.

"Mr. Brent's office," Suzie, his secretary, answered.

"Suzie, who was just in my office?"

"Mr. Brent. There you are. Ah, nobody's been in your office. Everyone is looking for you, sir. Are you all right? You don't sound well."

"Suzie, I think somebody is in my office. They just answered my phone. I want you to get corporate security to go in with you and check."

"Mr. Brent, I've been here all morning. There's nobody in

there. In fact, it's odd. You're the first person who's called all day."

"PLEASE!" Brent yelled. "Just check."

"Okay, okay. Hold on."

She put down the phone and came back on a moment later.

"No one is in there. Do you want me to call someone for you, Mr. Brent?"

"Tell Sam I know about Allied. Tell him to contact Ted Phillips. If he has to go to his office, tell him to go to his office. Tell him to let Ted know that whatever he thinks we're doing, we're not, I repeat, not, doing. A third party has become involved. Tell him that. Okay, Suzie? I'll be there in about an hour."

THE SECOND BRENT hung up, there was another ring. It came from the cell phone on his dresser, one of a special set of phones Guest had gotten him. It was a scrambler phone that would encrypt any conversation spoken over it. Guest had the other phone in the set. Brent walked over and picked it up.

"What?" Brent said.

"Robert? Guest. Just wanted to call and apprise you of the situation."

"Oh, did you?" Brent said. "And how is the situation going at this point?"

Guest paused at the agitation in Brent's tone.

"Very well. Everything's covered. What's going on?"

"Everything's covered, is it?" Brent said. "That's interesting. You want to hear something else interesting? Well, I just called my office and *I* answered the phone. You heard me. Someone said, 'Hello, Brent here.' And not only that, I just found out someone is actively fucking up my merger. Probably the same person who's pretending to be me. And if I had to hazard a guess, perhaps the same person who's blackmailing me. The one you just got through dealing with. Maybe you forgot to put that clause in your little negotiation session. No pretending to be me and no wrecking my merger! I don't know if you noticed, Mr. Guest, but those checks I gave you to smooth over this thing in El Salvador still haven't cleared. If I'm unable to salvage this deal, they never will."

Guest was unruffled.

"This somebody who answered your phone claiming to be you. What did he do after that? Hang up?"

"No. He said he knew about El Salvador, and then threatened he'd be seeing me soon. When I called back again, my secretary answered. I told her to check my office, but there was nobody there. In fact, she said nobody's called all day."

Guest began to laugh softly.

"I'm glad this is entertaining you."

"No, no," Guest said. "He works for the telephone company. Your blackmailer is a telephone man. I spoke to him earlier today."

"A telephone man," Brent said. "I thought you said they were cops."

"Yes. It seems they have a silent partner. This telephone employee must have disconnected your line and answered your phone from another location. And I suspect he's the one who was listening in on your line to start with."

"A phone guy is doing this to me?" Brent yelled. All the trouble he'd been put through. All the humiliation. These people who had manhandled him and shaken him down. Anger shot through him like a current. He considered what he was about to say. It'd be okay, he thought. The line he now was using was totally secure.

"I want you to take care of it, Mr. Guest. They've stepped over the line. I want these fuckers punished. Do you understand?"

There was a pause from Guest. Brent could almost hear his smile.

"Perfectly," Guest said.

Brent hung up.

What have I done?

He squelched the thought. No time. He lifted the phone back up again. He closed his eyes, thinking. He dialed Speed.

"Speed, listen up," Brent said when the banker answered. "Since Allied has already been put into play, is there any possibility of still getting it by going hostile?"

"Yes, there are some options, but they could be costly and we'd have to move right now. Tomorrow it'll be over."

There was no way to get board approval before then, Brent knew.

"Do it," Brent said. "Full bore. Any means necessary. Do you understand?"

"Perfectly," Speed said. Again, Brent thought he could hear a smile. Speed understood what Brent was doing. Telling him to go ahead without board approval was walking a wire over an inferno without a net.

"I'll call you back," Speed said.

Brent hung up an dialed his office again.

"Suzie," he said when his secretary picked up. "Contact the board members for an emergency meeting for six tonight."

Brent hung up.

He stood there still wet in his towel and wondered how it would all turn out. He watched Martine sleeping naked on the bed, her face and body like some pale vision he'd dreamed. Would he still be able to remember what she looked like in prison? He took in every detail of her, burning her image into his memory. He climbed back onto the bed. She stirred as he passed a hand through the black silk of her hair. He grabbed a fistful of it and yanked. She called out. He leaned into her until his mouth brushed the pink lobe of her ear.

"Don't you fucking move," he whispered.

CHAPTER TWENTY-SEVEN

MACKLIN SAT AS the train began to pull out of Grand Central. He dropped his now money-filled bag on the seat beside him. The teller at the bank had looked at him in stunned silence after he'd pushed the cash withdrawal slip under the bulletproof window. Whether at the amount, or that he possessed it, he wasn't sure. Even in hundreds, the eighty-seven thousand had turned out to be an encumbrance. He couldn't fit it in his pockets, so he had put it in the bag.

After a minute, the conductor came into the car and Macklin took out his wallet. He told the conductor "last stop," paid, and was handed his ticket. Only after the conductor left the car, did Macklin close his eyes. He remembered the bag then, and he reached over and propped it on his lap.

It was almost an hour and a half later when the conductor called out the last station and Macklin rose. Although he'd been up nearly twenty-four hours now, his attempt at rest had been fruitless. Only after he had Christina in a car would he feel safe enough to get some sleep. After they were on the move, they could pull over in a motel somewhere later tonight.

He got a cab at the station and instead of giving the driver his address, he told him to take him to the car rental place at the local strip mall. He rented a small sedan. He'd left his own car at his mother's house, but there was no way he was going back there to get it now. He pulled out and headed for his house. Twenty minutes later, he pulled into his driveway and parked beside Rose's car. He rushed up the path and went in.

"Hey, Rose," he called out. "Sorry about making you stay. You can go now."

Rose was on the telephone in the kitchen.

"Okay, he's here now. Thanks," she said, and hung up.

"Mr. Macklin. Finally. I just called your mother. The witness-protection people are looking for you. They came ten minutes ago. You have to call them."

Macklin stood completely still. He stared at her.

"They told me all about your brother and about the death threats," she continued. "They took Christina to a safe house. They want you to call so they can come back and pick you up."

Took Christina.

Macklin clutched the threshold to stop himself from falling.

"Mr. Macklin? Are you okay?"

He was too late. First Ray. Now Christina.

Macklin looked down. He felt cold and hollow suddenly, as if all the warmth inside him had just been sucked out of his body into the floor.

"It was the FBI?" he got out.

"That's right. A nice white-haired agent and his partner. They want you to call them. They left you this."

Macklin looked up. Rose was holding an envelope. He took it.

"I hope I did the right thing, Mr. Macklin."

"You did fine," Macklin said, not looking at her. "Why don't you go home now? I'll take care of things."

Rose collected her things and left. Macklin slid down the doorway to the floor. He waited until he heard her back out before he opened the letter. It was handwritten. The script impeccable.

We want you to get back together with Christina. Why don't you give us a call and we'll make arrangements. You remember the number, don't you?

P.S. You have a lovely home.

Macklin crumpled the note in his fist and withdrew his cell phone from his pocket with his other hand. He dialed his brother's cell phone number quickly. It was answered on the first ring.

"Sean?" Guest answered. He sounded pleased. "Home so soon? I'm sorry we just missed you. You're a worthy adversary, my friend. Your brother was good, but you are even better. I still can't figure out how you knew it was me in the car?

My voice? No, the whistling, right? Quite infectious, that Mr. Sinatra. Hard to get him out of your head once he gets in there. I'll have to remember that. And that little stunt with the phone in the car. Brilliant stuff. Not to mention the emergency brake on the train. And to lose me like that on the street. I tip my hat. No small honor. Honestly. I haven't had such fun in quite some time. My friend here is not quite as enthusiastic about you, but I think you can understand that. He is, after all, missing a thumb."

"You tell him that's not all he's gonna lose if he touches a hair on my wife's head," Macklin said.

"Oh, Sean," Guest said with a tinge of disappointment. "You've garnered my professional respect here. Don't blow it now with useless bravado. This is business. Let's make a deal."

"You want the copies," Macklin said.

"Hmmm. Good," Guest said, pleased again. "How enigmatic. 'The copies.' I like that. I'm beginning less and less to believe that any 'copies' exist, but a strong move. I'll go with it. You'll bring the copies and yourself, and I'll bring your wife, who I must say is quite exquisite, if a bit demure. There's a pay phone in the south parking lot of the Poughkeepsie Metro-North train station. In two hours when it rings, pick it up and we'll make our exchange. Again, Sean, my congratulations."

Guest hung up.

Macklin squeezed his eyes shut. The phone slipped from his fingers and went sliding along the kitchen floor.

They'd killed his brother and now they had his wife, and there was no way of getting her back. He'd tampered with things that were bigger than he was and made others pay the price. Two hours to call back, he thought. Two more hours and he and Christina would be going into a hole.

He looked down at the phone on the floor. There might be one chance. He rose up and ran for the basement door.

It took him less than two minutes to find his father's service pistol. It was in a toolbox on a shelf above his workbench, and he lifted it out and looked at it. It was an old, long-barreled .38, black iron with wood grips, cold and heavy in his hand. It had been part of his father's personal effects. Ray had told him to keep it after the funeral. He already had a gun, he'd said.

"You never know when you might need it."

Macklin tipped out the cylinder and took out the box of .38s. Then he loaded the chambers, slipped the gun into the outsize pocket of his work coat, and jumped up the stairs. He scooped the cell phone off the linoleum as he ran out of the house. He got into the car and backed out, screeching onto the main road.

Ten minutes later, he slammed to a stop in front of his local telephone central office. The first time he'd been here was to inquire about transferring from Manhattan. People were leaving the building now, shift change. He needed privacy to do what he needed to do, so he waited for them to file out. He sat in the car, tapping the steering wheel savagely.

He got out of his car as the last of the cars pulled from the gravel parking lot next to the building. He stepped to the plastic access box beside the steel door entrance and placed his electronic badge on top. There was a hum and the door clicked open. A security guard sat behind the front desk looking at him funny. He took out his ID card. The guard studied it closely.

"This is the Southern Duchess CO, right?" Macklin said.

"Yes," the guard said warily.

"I'm sorry," Macklin told him. "This is my second day. What floor is the frame on?"

The guard nodded now with understanding.

"It's on three," he said.

Macklin got on the elevator and pressed four. He jogged down the hall searching for the cellular office. He finally found it five minutes later on the second floor. There was a lock on the door, but its three-digit combination was written in pen on the wall next to it. Macklin punched the keys and went inside. He sat at the first terminal he came to and brought up the main menu for the cell program on the screen.

After Christina's accident, he'd been assigned to the Midtown cellular office for a few weeks. Cell sites, he'd learned, were receiver-transmitters set up throughout a given area. When you dialed a cellular phone, a signal went out to all of an area's sites simultaneously. Because some sites overlapped, every site that could detect your signal responded. Then, a split-second signal-strength comparison was made among them. Whichever had the strongest signal would make the connection. It was possible, Macklin knew, to get a rough idea of where the phone you were calling was physically located by comparing signal strengths and site locations, a process called triangulation. Police had come in one day for help in tracking down some cell phone pirates.

Macklin brought up the test command. He typed in his brother's cell phone number and hit *enter*. Dial tone came from the computer speaker, followed by the high-pitched jingle of the phone number, and then there were some beeps followed by static. Then a series of letters and numbers followed by percentages appeared on the screen. They represented the cell-site locations followed by their strengths. He clicked *print*, and a loud chattering began a few desks down.

He stepped to the printer and ripped out the sheet.

With the paper in his hand, he walked over to the wide, metal filing cabinet in the corner of the long room. The heavy drawer rolled out smoothly.

Inside were huge, laminated maps of the area. He lifted one out and laid it on a desk. Along with roads and terrain, numbers and letters were typed all over it. This was the cell-site map. He checked the numbers on the map against the ones on the page. With a marker he took from the desk, he circled the three strongest sites that had picked up the signal for his brother's phone. Then he drew an X in the center of them.

As far as he could tell, Ray's cell phone was located somewhere within a three-mile area a little north of Poughkeepsie, about twenty miles west from where he stood.

And so was his wife.

He sped back to the terminal and tested his brother's phone again. He compared the new test numbers with the ones on the paper. They matched exactly. They were stopped somewhere, holding her out of sight away from the train station until the exchange.

He cleared the screen, then wiped the map and put it away quickly. He ran out the door, down the corridor, and took the stairs. He slowed in the lobby as he passed the guard. Then he jumped back in the car, started it up, and peeled out, heading west.

CHAPTER TWENTY-EIGHT

IT WAS COMING on evening when Scully pulled off the highway back into the Bronx, and rolled down the block under the El. He stopped at a red light next to the ballpark where he'd first played little league. A garbage bag blew across the packed dust and stuck fast in the rusting backstop. He shook his head.

You should be in Florida drinking piña coladas, he thought.

He'd awoken that morning from a nightmare in which Carlita and Juan were yelling for help in the upstairs window of a burning house. He was standing beneath the window and told Carlita to drop Juan to him. When she did, the baby passed right through his fingers to the cement. Ray appeared beside him wearing a fireman's hat and coat. "Nice try, sucker," he'd said.

Scully had checked out of the Baltimore hotel room and driven. Instead of heading for the train station, he found himself back on the highway heading back the way he'd come. In the hotel where he'd left Carlita, the clerk told him she'd already checked out. He figured she'd head back to her old apartment, so he'd crossed back over the bridge.

Twenty minutes later, he was at Carlita's apartment building. He watched the empty street for ten minutes before he got out. He went in the front door, up the stairs, and knocked on her door. Somebody peeked out the security hole, and the door opened.

Carlita stood there, holding a bucket of water. There was a sponge on the floor where she'd been trying to clean up the blood.

"Jimmy!" she cried.

She hugged him tightly.

Scully looked at the room. The plastic she'd put over the broken window. The bullet holes in the wall.

"Carlita, get Juan," Scully said. "Come on. We're going."

"*Viajar?*"

"*Sí,*" Scully said. "Far, far away. C'mon. Get Juan."

He grabbed her suitcase and the baby bag. She picked up the swaddled baby, and they left and went down to the car. When he turned to her, she was looking back at the tenement and crying. He thought that she was somehow already missing the malevolent place, but then figured it out.

"Yeah," Scully said. "I know. I miss him, too."

They got on the highway. Scully planned as he drove. There was a little suburb outside of Baltimore near the water that was quiet and nice. He'd lived around there when he'd played ball and thought it might be nice to go back. Get a little place. Maybe a job coaching high school. Set Carlita up with something nice. It was a pipe dream, probably, but reality meant he'd have to turn himself in and he wasn't about to do that.

Five minutes later, he passed the neighborhood he'd grown up in, for the last time. A blur of old buildings and cracked concrete. Rust. Ten minutes after that he slowed slightly as Yankee Stadium rose up on the left.

"So long," he said.

CHAPTER TWENTY-NINE

IT WAS ALMOST full dark when Macklin found the car. He'd been through the parking lots of three motels in the search area and found nothing. After scanning a fourth without spotting the blue sedan, he was ready to return to the central office for another search. But as he was pulling out, he noticed a rundown minimall on the opposite side of the parkway. Something told him to take a look. There behind a closed supermarket was the car.

Guest's Crown Victoria.

Macklin pulled up beside it slowly. He scanned the area around the car thoroughly, wrapped a hand around the pistol in his pocket, and got out. When he peered in the window, he could see the bloodstains on the backseat.

Breath labored in and out of his lungs.

Okay, he thought, taking a step back. What did that mean?

It meant Guest and the one he'd cut had hidden their car here and were in the motel across the road, he decided.

But what could he do? They had taken out Ray and he had been a seasoned cop.

He took a breath.

He had to get Christina. Surprise was his only chance. He walked quickly back to his car with the gun bouncing off his thigh.

He made a U-turn and turned right, following the road in front of the stores. Besides the empty supermarket, there was a pizza shop and a liquor store and a karate place. A McDonald's stood by itself on the corner. The businesses seemed tired and slightly run-down, as if they had been replaced by something better recently. A few people were walking in the parking lot to and from the stores. People stopping off from work, grabbing takeout. It seemed absurd to him that normal life could go on while his wife was being held across the street. He slowed for a man in a suit who crossed in front of him. Macklin noticed the blond crew cut and the big white bandage as the big man pulled open the glass door of the McDonald's and stepped inside.

The car rocked violently forward as his foot dropped on the brake.

The tires screeched as he made a U-turn.

He drove back around until he was facing the glass windows of the front of the restaurant. There were a few people standing by the counter, looking up at selections, and beyond them, he could see crew cut sitting at a small table.

Macklin remembered the man's lighter. He's a SEAL. He'll fuckin' kill me.

Macklin watched, transfixed, as the big man stood and walked out of sight to the side of the restaurant. Macklin drove to the right and watched him pass down a corridor toward the back, open a door, and step in. Macklin pulled forward quickly and stopped.

Now or never, he thought.

He got out and found himself jogging quickly for the side door, palming the gun. He stepped into the restaurant and passed by the empty plastic booths. He took the gun out and took a short breath and pulled the door for the bathroom.

There was no one at the sink or at the urinal, and he crouched and saw the feet beneath the stall door. There was Muzak playing The Police's "Roxanne" in tepid jazz. There was a lock on the outside door, and he clicked it shut. Then he brought up his leg and kicked in the stall door.

The SEAL sat looking up at him in complete surprise.

Macklin had the gun two inches between the man's eyes and was about to ask where his wife was when the man rose up.

Macklin squeezed the trigger.

Click.

Nothing.

The SEAL smiled as he jumped up and hit him with an uppercut left that brought Macklin up on his tippy-toes. He followed through with a right elbow to the cheek, which knocked Macklin out of the stall and right on his ass.

"Thought you'd do me in with that old hog iron?" the SEAL said, casually buckling up his pants and stepping out of the stall. He grabbed Macklin by his hair and dragged him back in.

"Well, I'll give you an E for effort," he said, trying to force Macklin's head into the bowl.

Macklin grabbed the rancid wet rim and resisted for all he was worth. The SEAL cracked Macklin's forehead off the porcelain rim and dropped him beside it. Macklin's whole body felt like rubber as he heard the SEAL taking something out. There was a click of metal.

Macklin lay there bleeding. Maybe this was for the best. Then he thought of his wife all alone in the room. He pushed up on his hands and kicked back. His foot caught the stall door, and it flew back and hit on something. There was a yell and a cough, and the tile beside Macklin's head exploded in a shower of fragments. Macklin found his feet and threw himself back. He banged into the SEAL, turned, and put both hands on the gun.

The SEAL head-butted him, but he wouldn't let go. The SEAL tried to knee him in the balls, but he blocked it with his thigh. Macklin let one hand off the gun and brought a fist down on the SEAL's injured hand, catching it on the sink. He could feel strength pass from the SEAL, and he pointed the gun in toward the SEAL's body. He wrapped a finger around the trigger and pulled.

A splatter came with the cough this time, and the SEAL slid down under the urinal.

Blood was everywhere, on the white tile walls, in the sink, pooled thick on the floor. Its warm copper smell clogged the close air. Macklin fell on one knee and wretched. He wiped his mouth and looked at the dead SEAL.

Christina, he thought. Had to get Christina.

He lifted up the SEAL's gun, a heavy .357 with a silencer. He dropped it in his pocket. He stuffed his father's old gun in his pants. He went quickly through the SEAL's pockets. He found car keys, a speedloader for the revolver, a pair of handcuffs, and a key on a wooden chain that had "14" carved into it.

He stood and peeked out the door. There was still no one sitting along this narrow part of the restaurant. Soft oboes continued to destroy "Roxanne." Macklin stepped out and jogged quickly for the door and ran for his car.

He drove onto the parkway and got off at the next exit south. He crossed over the parkway on a bridge and headed back up a side street for the motel. He parked his car a quarter mile up from the motel alongside the fence of some darkened electrical station. He shut off the engine and got out.

It was pitch black as he walked along the wooded road. He went into the trees when he saw headlights approach and continued toward the motel. He started to run after a while. Guest would be getting suspicious about the SEAL not returning, he knew. He reached the motel and reloaded all the chambers of the .357 with rounds from the speedloader. Macklin stood there for a moment, staring at the yellow lights of the motel through the black bars of trees. Then he stepped down the ridge to get his wife.

Fourteen was the last room on the end of the motel's low, thin structure. Its lights were off. He approached slowly and stopped in front of the door. Should he wait? Go around back? He didn't have time. He took out the .357 and the key and held his breath. With painstaking slowness, he slipped the key into the lock on the doorknob. No, he decided, before turning it. He needed a distraction. There was an old metal lawn chair in front of the room's picture window. Macklin lifted it up, took a step back, and threw it at the window. Then he rushed the door and turned the knob, glass crashing.

In the darkened room, he trained his gun at a figure standing completely still beside the decimated window. Macklin's hand found the wall switch and flicked it on. It was Guest. The whole front of his white dress shirt was stained black with blood. He had a gun in his hand, but it was up at his throat with his other hand trying in vain to staunch the wound. His eyes were wide and white. He beamed them at Macklin.

Guest stumbled forward. He began to bring his gun down slowly to his side.

Over now, Macklin thought.

Macklin was waiting for the gun to drop out of Guest's hand when it suddenly went off.

Macklin pulled the trigger of his .357 a second after, and the bullet bit into Guest's chest and he dropped onto the carpet.

Macklin turned toward the back of the room. There was a bed against the wall with a slight shape under the cover. He stepped up and pulled back the sheet. His wife lay on her side with her eyes open.

"Christina," he said.

She tipped forward when he put his hand on her. There was a fist-sized opening in her back, and she was lying in blood.

No.

He lay down with her for a moment, hugging her. He buried his face in her neck.

Not you.

He rose, lifting her. He carried her outside.

There were police cars at the McDonald's across the parkway, their flashers spinning blue and red. He stepped with his wife away from the motel up into the trees.

* * *

IT WAS TWENTY minutes later when he pulled up in front of his house. He brought her back to her room and laid her down on the bed and got in next to her. He remembered the day they met eight years ago. It was on a service road, two blocks away from his apartment, that he came across her. All light and beauty shimmering on the cracked asphalt like a mirage. She had the hood of her new car up.

"Can I help you?" he'd said.

Her car wouldn't start, she said, and she'd called AAA, but that had been over an hour ago.

"Mind if I took a look?"

He got in and turned the key, but nothing happened. Then he noticed that she'd left it in gear, so he put it in park, tried it again, and it started right up.

She had wanted to pay him.

"I don't want money," he'd said, looking at her and smiling, "but I could use a ride."

He remembered how she'd looked at him then for a long moment, her blue crystalline eyes piercing so starkly into his own that he had to look away, the warmth that shivered through his heart when she smiled suddenly.

"Okay, " she'd said. "Hop in."

Hop in, he thought.

He recalled those times, lying with her on the beach at night that first summer. The sound of the waves and the warm breeze. Her warm skin and the stars, bright in the endless night.

Hop in.

They'd come for him any moment now. The police or whoever. Somebody had to have gotten his plate. He lay there waiting. Then he sat up quickly, realizing there was one thing left undone.

One last visit needed to be paid.

Macklin stood. He was covered in blood, and he took off his clothes and went to his closet and took out new ones. When he was dressed, he walked over to his wife and closed her eyelids with his fingers. He placed a kiss on her forehead, cool now.

He walked out of the room and through the house and out the front door. He locked the house up tight and went down the steps.

In the front yard, he stood looking out for a moment. Black sky, the dark field across, the bleak, leafless trees. He got in the car, started it up, and flicked on the headlights. Then he peeled out into the road in a squeal of tires, heading south.

CHAPTER THIRTY

BRENT SIPPED HIS champagne and peered out tinted glass at the passing lights. In the soft, black leather beside him, Martine put her head on his shoulder and slid her fine-boned hand into his own. Unbelievable, he thought. This morning he was convinced he'd never see her again. But now, he thought. Now.

He'd actually pulled it off. Speed had done his magic and they'd accomplished a hostile takeover. It ended up costing more than Brent had expected, but at the emergency meeting, the board had granted its grudging acceptance to the deal. And not only that, one hundred eighty million dollars in stock options were now his. Since they'd gone to such drastic measures, Speed had taken the liberty of setting up a personal deal for him even more lucrative than the original.

How ironic, he thought. The man who'd attempted to wreck his deal had ended up only making it all the sweeter.

Brent smiled and drank more champagne.

What a day.

Lord knew, it'd been messy.

Right after the emergency meeting, Brent had spotted the newspaper on Suzie's desk. The headline "COP SHOT" above a picture of the man who'd shaken him down. He'd been terrified until he went through the article and read that the man had been suspected of drug theft and a cartel was thought responsible. It didn't take a brain surgeon to know it'd been Guest. He was surprised to note that without the threat of getting caught, he was basically all right with it. If he wanted to be totally truthful, he might admit to feeling a little thrilled.

Hadn't he only done what needed to be done?

He hadn't ordered anyone killed in El Salvador, but no matter how it came out, the media would've made him responsible. His life's work, his merger, would've been irrevocably destroyed. Not only would Allied not want to deal with him, no biotech would. He'd been made to solve problems that were simply impossible. What was he supposed to do, bend over? No way. He wouldn't go down without a fight.

The cop had started it, humiliating him, putting his hands on him, extorting funds.

Guest had just ended what had to be stopped.

But even that portion of this whole thing was over now.

Half an hour ago, Guest had called to say he'd caught up with the cop's brother. The one who'd fucked with him in the first place. Brent couldn't get over that a phone guy had almost ruined him. He could've accepted being surveilled by the government. Even some rival company. But by some schmuck? It was insulting.

He'd be seeing another face in the paper tomorrow morning, he thought.

Martine put her hand on his thigh.

It was okay. He was on a different level now. He could feel it.

After Guest had reassured him that the tape Brent had was the only one in existence, he'd hung up and smashed it open with the heel of his shoe. Then he'd burned the ribbon and washed its ashes down the sink.

He told Martine to get dressed and he'd hired a limousine. Now they were on their way to Mitch's apartment to pick him up.

Time to celebrate.

They drove down Fifth. Brent looked out at the white granite residences. You could tell by their stateliness, by the white-gloved doormen who stood beneath their hunter green canopies, that the lives lived within them were better, more exciting, grander. Some things were not subject to doubt. He smiled. He'd call a broker Monday morning.

The car slowed at a building and stopped.

"What's first on the agenda?" Mitch asked, piling into the car with his date.

"Now, now," Brent said, shaking his hand, "don't spoil the surprise."

"This here's Gina," Mitch said.

Gina was a tall, large-breasted blonde. Brent looked at Martine. Her contempt was palpable in the darkness beside him.

The restaurant was somewhere down in SoHo. They had

more champagne in the car, and Brent was already buzzing when they stepped onto the sidewalk. Brent gave his name, and menus were conjured and they were led forward. They were seated at a corner table. The dark place was lit by parchment-covered lanterns. White blossoms seemed to be everywhere above and around them in the soothing dark, like suspended ticker tape in an elegant parade. There were models about, both men and women. You could see them all around, sitting at couches, standing up at the bar. Everybody seemed young and rich and thin. The winners, Brent thought. Brent raised a glass.

"To us," he said.

The dinner was long and high-spirited. They finished three bottles of wine. Even Martine's deep Gallic contempt seemed to lift in the rarefied atmosphere. Brent paid and left an enormous tip.

They thanked the maître d' and walked out to the waiting limo.

"Max's," Mitch told the driver.

Max's was a club far uptown that Brent had only heard of. It was actually in Spanish Harlem, but there was a tremendous amount of security or something. A favorite of celebrities and socialites alike. Mitch took out a black leather satchel and unzipped it. Inside were a mirror, a razor, a metal straw, and a glass vial of pinkish powder.

Brent was stunned.

"Are you crazy?" he said. Brent hadn't done coke since he'd gone to the Palladium when he was what? Twenty-five?

"Oh, you said we were partying tonight, Robert. We're gonna do it right," Mitch said, dangling the vial from its little silver chain.

Martine clapped her hands and giggled like a little girl.

She cocked a dark eyebrow at Mitch and smiled.

"I've finally found a reason to like you, Meetch," she said in her sultry voice.

Mitch tapped out some cocaine and took two quick hits. They all took turns. Gina racked two monster lines with the dexterity of a chemist and inhaled them. She gave Brent a smile and a lingering half-lidded stare along with the mirror and straw. Brent laid out two lines for Martine and watched her bend down her long graceful neck, squint her eyes, and hit them. There was a soft, innocent quality to the way she did it, a deer at a salt lick. Brent tapped out some for himself and consumed it. He felt the euphoria almost immediately. He looked out at the steadily worsening streets, feeling power course through him.

They slowed by what looked like a warehouse. There was a line of limousines there already and a crowd by a dingy door. When Brent stepped out, he could see the place wasn't a warehouse, but some inner-city department store. A place where third-world people purchased three-dollar shirts and five-dollar sneakers. Brent smiled out at the millionaires behind the velvet rope beside it.

Mitch gave the bouncer a name and they were let in. They went down some rancid steps and through a door. The place was mobbed. Dance music pounded. They weren't the only ones here from the restaurant they'd just left, it seemed, because all around were more of the young and beautiful and rich, dancing and smoking. Perfect teeth glowed in the strobe light.

They went to the bar and to the unisex bathroom and back to the bar. Brent came back from the bathroom alone one time to find some long-haired, Eurotrash pretty boy in a silk suit talking into Martine's ear. Without saying anything, Brent walked up and gave the guy a hard little head butt to the cheek.

"Jesus Christ, I'm sorry," Brent yelled in mock apology, holding the guy by his elbow. "Are you all right? Let me buy you a beer."

The Eurotrash looked at him in distress. He tapped at where Brent had struck him, checking it in the mirror behind the bar, and quickly left.

Mitch gave Brent a high five. They laughed together. Brent smiled at his friend. He could feel the otherness that he'd carried around with him all his life start to melt away. He and this man who'd been born into privilege were friends finally, true equals. Brent had arrived, he realized. He could let himself accept it now.

"Yes," Martine whispered in Brent's ear. "Fight like dogs over me."

They drank. After a while, they went out onto the dance floor. They went to the unisex bathroom at least three more times. The last time, it was just he and the two girls. Gina rubbed Martine's back with her long, red-nailed hands as she snorted. Brent watched with an excitement bordering on mortal terror as Martine grabbed Gina's hand and brought it down to her ass.

Martine wiped her nose and giggled when she saw Brent's face in the mirror.

"Yes, Robert?" Martine said. She took a step and grabbed Gina's breasts from behind. She rested her head softly on Gina's shoulder.

"Is this what you like?" she asked provocatively, and then burst into laughter.

Brent breathed slowly, rapt in the two sets of black-rimmed eyes.

Martine grabbed Gina's hand and took her out the door. Brent followed.

They got Mitch and went out of the club and back to the limo.

"Back to Fifth," Mitch told the driver.

The five-minute trip went by in tense silence. They pulled up to Mitch's apartment on Fifth.

"I have a flight tomorrow. I gotta get some sleep," Mitch said. "Night, Martine. Night, Gina," he said.

Brent grabbed Mitch's arm.

"Isn't Gina going with you?"

Mitch put a hand to the back of Brent's head.

"Don't say I never did anything for you," he said, handing him the vial of coke.

"Where to, sir?" asked the driver.

Brent looked at the two women sitting across from him.

He gave the chauffeur his address.

CHAPTER THIRTY-ONE

IT WAS WELL after midnight when Macklin slowed by Brent's First Avenue building in his phone truck. When he'd pulled into the garage earlier, his gang had already been dispatched and the foreman was somewhere upstairs. He'd told the guard he was late and went to his truck and pulled out. He'd been by the central office, and although Brent's home number was unlisted, after an hour of searching through the system, he found it. The CEO's address had come with the number. For the apartment number, it just said "15," which Macklin thought was a misprint until it dawned on him that the CEO's apartment must consist of the whole of the fifteenth floor.

Macklin circled the block. When he saw the construction site catty-corner to Brent's building on Fifty-second Street, he pulled to the curb, flicked on the overhead strobes, and got out.

He opened the back of the truck, got an empty tool bucket, and put the gun in it. He took out tin snips, a flashlight, some strong rubber tape, rags, some rubber cord. He took down the ladder, picked up the bucket, and put on his old, worn helmet. Then he got out of the truck and walked toward the fence.

He put the ladder against the fence and climbed up. He pointed the flashlight's beam down into the construction site. Cruciform I-beams rose from the exposed, dark earth. Wood and rebar were stacked over by the corner to his right.

He managed to stay upright as he went down the debris pile. They'd poured most of the foundation, and he walked along its concrete ridge until he came to the back of Brent's building. There were a few strands of razor wire along the stone wall separating the site from the building's courtyard. He took out the snips and cut them down.

As he climbed over the fence, he could smell garbage from a nearby archway, and he headed toward it. His flashlight illuminated a long row of slick, black plastic bags beside a thick metal-plated door. He walked to the door and yanked it open. Inside was a closed metal gate. He peered through the grid of metal into the basement. Lights were on, and there was the high whine of machinery coming from the left. To the right, he could make out the open door of a service elevator. The light inside it was off, and there was no night serviceman to worry about. The basement was empty. There'd just be a doorman, far away in the upstairs lobby.

He tried the gate, but it was locked. He looked down and saw that a square metal plate had been welded to the door next to the lock to protect it from being jimmied. He put his head to the grate and saw the pushbar on the other side. There was some space underneath the door, so he took off his coat and bent down. He could get his arm under the door up to the bicep, but it wasn't enough to reach up and push the bar. He sat thinking. He'd need something strong and skinny to force the bar. He opened the outside door again.

When he came back, he was carrying a three-foot piece of rebar from the construction site. He lay down on the floor and slid it under the door. It took twenty minutes to finally put enough pressure on the bar to force the pushbar. The door slipped open. He got up and stepped toward the elevator.

It was an old manual job, without any buttons, just a worn, wooden push handle to make it go. He took the hook off the door, slid its gate closed, and pushed the wooden handle smoothly forward. The elevator started and began sliding up.

He left the light off, counting the floors. The elevator kicked off by itself at the top. He looked at the lock on the door. It was double-sided, the kind that needs keys for both sides, but the body of the lock was on the wrong side, held to the shaft door with Phillips-head screws. The super had been trying to make a few bucks probably, or some fly-by-night locksmith. Macklin took out his Leatherman, clicked open the screwdriver, and went to work. In five minutes, he was finished. Although the lock was still firmly closed, it was no longer attached to the door.

Macklin put his ear to the door and heard only silence. He took the gun from the bucket, slid the door open, hooked it, and stepped into the darkened apartment.

He went to the right and walked quietly down a narrow,

carpeted hall. At the end of it was a partially closed door from which music and some high-pitched giggling emanated. He raised the pistol as he approached.

Macklin peered in from the hallway. What he saw brought him pause. A shirtless blonde woman was kissing another woman at the end of a large bed.

What the fuck? Lesbians?

In the hall, Macklin tensed. Was he in the wrong apartment? The wrong building?

A man yelled from out of sight.

"Robert!" one of them said.

The man of the house, Macklin thought.

The two women stopped kissing. Macklin took a few steps back. The women spoke to each other and seemed to be consulting with the unseen man. They got off the bed and walked out of sight. A door closed. Then Macklin stepped forward into the room with the gun raised.

Brent was lying back on the bed, wiping his nose. His pants were around his ankles and he was wearing boxer shorts. His dress shirt was unbuttoned to the waist. His red-rimmed eyes turned slowly toward Macklin. Then they widened. Macklin sighted between them and pulled back the hammer on the revolver with his thumb, a small but distinct metal clack above the stereo.

Macklin took in the mound of coke on the mirror on the dresser and gestured with the gun for Brent to get up. Brent just lay there, stunned. Macklin moved the gun slightly and squeezed the trigger. The gun coughed and the pillow beside Brent's head exploded in a burst of feathers. Brent hopped instantly to his feet, pulling up his pants, and came quickly around the bed. Macklin gestured again at the door, and Brent walked toward it. Macklin was going to break the knob on the bathroom door to lock the girls in, but then decided he didn't need to.

He followed Brent into the hall.

"That way," he said, gesturing back toward the hall he'd just come down.

"Wait. You're, um, a phone guy, right?" Brent said as he walked.

"Elevator," Macklin said as they came to it. Brent stepped in.

"You know," he said nervously. "Those girls, they . . . they'd do whatever you . . . um. They listen to me. Couldn't we come to . . . you want money?"

Macklin pressed the gun hard between Brent's eyes, pushing his head against the elevator's metal wall.

"Down," he said.

Brent just stood there.

"I don't, I don't know how."

Macklin clouted him twice across the head with the barrel of the gun. Brent cried out, then grasped the handle shutting the door and pushed the handle making the elevator descend.

"See?" Macklin said. "You do know."

In the basement, Macklin took tape from his bucket and bound Brent's hands behind him. Macklin took off his jacket and draped it on Brent's back to hide the tape. Then, he prodded him along, bringing him out the back door. As Macklin led him past the garbage, Brent started to cry. Macklin clicked back the revolver's hammer in Brent's ear.

"Make a sound," he said, "and I'm gonna shoot you."

Brent whimpered and nodded his head.

There was some traffic passing on First Avenue, but there

was no one on the sidewalk. They banged through the metal service gate. Macklin led Brent around the corner to the truck and opened the back. He made Brent get in, sat him down, and taped his feet. He chucked the tool bucket inside, looked over by the fence, and saw his ladder still there. He went and got it and threw it in on top of Brent.

Macklin locked up, got into the cab, and started the engine.

"You know, I'm not even like that," Brent called from the back. "The coke and those . . . everything. I . . ."

Macklin put the truck in drive.

"Save your breath," he said.

Macklin was going to turn off the strobe lights, but fuck it. This was an emergency.

He laid the gun on the seat beside him, narrowed his eyes, and stepped hard on the gas.

IN THE BACK of the truck, Brent was panicking.

The pain in his head from where Macklin had hit him was staggering. There would be more pain, he knew. Torture. He could feel his breath coming more rapidly. He'd hyperventilate soon, probably suffocate. His face was pressed against the cold, filthy floor of the truck. When they hit a bump, something sharp stuck into his back.

Calm. He had to calm himself. It was the coke, he knew. Mixed with adrenaline, making it impossible for him to think. What to do? From every story he'd ever heard about war, every example of victory under fire, it was the man who kept his head who won. The man who stood and aimed. The man who stayed cool. That's what was needed. He had to take a moment to collect himself.

The truck bumped again, and there was another stabbing pain in his side as he slid around in the truck. He'd fucking bleed to death before they stopped. He reached around behind him, probed with his fingers, and found a sharp, bent-up corner of some metal housing. He maneuvered himself until he got his taped wrists beside it. He couldn't move his arms, so he began to rock back and forth, digging his wrists in to get at the tape. The truck bumped again, and his hand went wet and sticky. He could feel the sting where his arm had been opened up, but he couldn't stop. He had to get this done. Moving back and forth, he didn't know if it was skin or tape he was cutting. All he knew was that he had to get his hands free or he'd die.

MACKLIN DROVE OVER to Lex and made a left and then drove down to Thirty-ninth and made a right. He drove a block to Park Avenue South and made another right, pointing the truck dead set at the gargantuan tower of the MetLife Building. He came to where the avenue split at the viaduct, and instead of going up, he veered to the right and down. He slowed by the secret vault door and came to a stop.

He hopped out of the cab. There was a folded tent in the attic space above the cab, and he grabbed it and brought it out. He unfolded it on the street and tied the flaps to the doors and roof of the truck. Then he slit the side of the tent by the vault door and took out his key and opened the door. He opened the doors of the truck and slid Brent forward. He got a rag and stuffed it in the CEO's mouth and secured it with a tight wrap of tape. Then he tied another rag tight around his eyes. He grabbed a set of bolt cutters and a flashlight. He cut the tape from Brent's feet with his shears, lifted him up by the back of his dress shirt, and led him through the tent and into the underground door.

Macklin shut the door behind him. He turned on the flashlight and pushed Brent down the corridor before him. When they came to the two doors, instead of taking out his keys and unlocking the telephone door on his right, Macklin lifted the bolt cutters off his shoulder and chopped through the lock of the water department door on the left. The door creaked inward on rusty hinges, and Macklin pushed the CEO in.

This chamber had a lower ceiling than the telephone vault. There was coolness, a dampness in the closed air. Macklin passed the light over some old machinery. There was a row of huge motors beside consoles with strange wooden handles, turn wheels, and dials with faded hand-painted numbers behind the glass.

Past this machinery, in the floor, was a wood-covered circle about six feet in diameter. It was hinged on one side, and there was a lock on it. Macklin put Brent on his knees beside it, lowered the bolt cutters, and bit the lock in two. He threw the cover up and back. As it clattered loudly in the blackness of the room, a small voice told him that he didn't have to do this, that it had gone far enough. Then he thought of his brother and his wife, and he told the voice to go fuck itself.

He was turning around to grab Brent when he was tackled to the floor.

BRENT GRABBED THE gun out of Macklin's waistband. He stood and pointed it against Macklin's head.

Macklin froze.

Brent hit him with the gun. He caught him in the temple,

and Macklin did a stutter step, lost his feet, and sat. Brent kicked a wing tip into his throat. Macklin gagged and curled up into a fetal position.

"You think you can come into my house?" Brent roared. He kicked Macklin in the ribs this time. "My house?"

Brent raised the gun. Yes, he thought. He could do even this. He took a step back, so he wouldn't be splattered with any blood, and then he was falling.

There was darkness and damp, and he was picking up speed, terrible speed. He knew he'd be dead in a second, but he was still falling. He watched the circle of pale, receding light that was the world above steadily getting smaller and smaller.

From out of his panic, flashes of memory came to him then. Ones, oddly enough, not of the city he'd fought so hard to make a place in, but of the home he'd tried so hard to leave behind. A tire swing beneath an ancient pine tree. A muscle car with rusting rocker panels in the dirt yard before a trailer. An ill-kept ball field beside a slow, brown river. His father's tar-caked boots on the old, listing porch. A winter storm approaching over dark, distant mountains.

Then everything went black in a vaporizing explosion of cold.

CHAPTER THIRTY-TWO

MACKLIN SAT THERE wheezing. His throat was on fire where Brent had kicked him. It felt like someone was grinding crushed glass into his temple when he moved his head. He crawled to the rim of the hole and looked down.

It was pitch black. A cool breeze came up from it. He thought he might've heard a faint sound far beneath, but he wasn't sure. A feeling of vertigo gripped him then, and he backed quickly. He got to his feet and picked up the light. He found the wood cover and put it back on carefully. He picked up his bolt cutters and stepped for the chamber door.

He tried to close the water department door, but it kept coming open. He finally took the lock and chain from the phone vault door and locked it shut. There was a loud thump of a car on the roadway above, and he walked down the corridor for the street.

He opened the door and stepped outside into the tent. He peeked out of its side at the night street, but it was empty. There weren't even any cars now. He watched the traffic lights trip down the empty avenue in a sweep, as if at the beck of some passing unseen hand.

It took him five minutes to break the tent down. He put it back in its proper place and locked the truck. He got into the cab, shut off the emergency lights, and put it in drive.

He stopped before Grand Central. He rolled down the window, pulled the side mirror in, and looked at himself. His temple was bleeding. It would scar just like the one on the other side, he knew.

He thought of his wife then, his brother. He began to cry and stopped himself. Then he began to cry again.

He looked up at the stark, massive buildings around him. In the back of the truck was a cable cutter, and for a moment, looking up at those unfeeling towers, he felt like getting it and taking it back into the vault. He felt like whacking the cables, cutting the lines, shutting it down. If he hurried, he could probably make it down to Wall Street by daylight.

But others would just come to fix it, he knew. Put in lines that were better and faster. Just as others would come to take Brent's place. The world would move on, no matter what he did, crushing and grinding on and on without account.

He sat there for a long time. There was traffic after a while. Garbage trucks and newspaper trucks passing on Forty-second Street before him. Old cars towing tin doughnut shacks. Street sweepers hissing at the curbs. A police car passed by slowly, the cop in the passenger seat stretching his arms in a yawn.

People eventually began to emerge into the gray glow of first light from the subways. Men, women, deli workers and nannies and shift workers. A sleepy army of caretakers converging onto a city that cared nothing for them.

Macklin banged the mirror back into place with the heel of his hand and put the truck into drive. He pulled out and made a left and rolled westward. He picked up speed as he crossed the massive avenues. He looked back once in his west coast mirror. The backlit Midtown towers in the graying sky were like dark judges ringed round. Then he turned his gaze forward through the dusty windshield and stepped down hard on the gas, fleeing the coming of the sun.

ACKNOWLEDGMENTS

THIS BOOK COULD not have been completed without the help and support of the following people:

Mary, Keelan, Cara, and Brynna.

Danny Miller, for getting me the job.

Harlan Ellison.

Tom and Molly Broussard.

Morgan Entrekin and Judith Curr.

George Lucas, for his keen editorial work as well as his gracious tolerance of my status as a Luddite.

Lori and Sarah, for not only being two of the nicest people in the world, but for going all out for my benefit.

Richard, for coming out of the corner swinging all fifteen-plus rounds, from the book's inception to its completion.

And finally, Jim, for one full year of the "good life." It was pretty damn cool.